NO GOOD REASON

MARG MCALISTER

Blue Gem Publishing

This edition published by Blue Gem Publishing in 2022.

Title: No Good Reason | Marg McAlister, author

ISBN: 978-1-922772-97-8 (Paperback edition)

ISBN: 978-0-9924403-7-4 (Ebook edition)

Cover Design by Annie Moril

V05042022

An Elusive Client

THEY'D BEEN PADDLING for hours, and there was still no sign of what they sought.

Georgie pushed her sunglasses more firmly onto her nose against the glare of the sun glinting off the waters of Sussex Inlet and glanced across at the man paddling next to her with smooth, even strokes.

How things change, she thought. A scant year ago, working for her father at his RV Empire in Indiana, she had never heard of Scott Mowbray. Now, she couldn't imagine life without him. She'd left behind her beloved gypsy trailer—well, *replica* gypsy trailer—and rapidly adapted to life in a well-equipped off-road rig, touring Scott's home country of Australia.

What she *hadn't* left behind was her crystal ball or the tendency to attract people who needed her unique insights to help them solve their problems. It had taken her a while to admit that she had indeed inherited her great-grandma Rosa's gift of the Sight, as well as her crystal ball, but finally, she could no longer deny what she was. Twelve months of wandering the USA, most of it with Scott, had seen her fall naturally into being a kind of psychic detective before heading off overseas to meet his family.

The thought made her grin wryly. *Psychic detective. Gypsy fortune-teller.* It sounded ridiculous.

And yet, here she was, with almost a year behind her of using the crystal ball to help people who needed her. One of the hardest things to explain was how she was, in some strange way, *drawn* to them, like iron filings to a magnet.

Lulled by the sun on her back and the gentle slap of water on the hull of her kayak, Georgie lay her paddle across her lap and closed her eyes for a moment, drifting on the current while she listened to the warbling call of a currawong flying overhead.

A light breeze on her face, the smell of the outdoors, and nothing to do but relax. *Bliss.* This morning had been perfect, cruising the canals of Sussex Inlet with Scott, gliding past houses with stretches of lawn sweeping down to private jetties, waving at people working in their gardens or reading in deckchairs.

The only thing was, they still hadn't found what she was looking for, and now she was beginning to wonder if they would. Yet the crystal ball was rarely wrong. It could be cryptic, yes…but the same image two nights in a row?

She could still see the picture clearly in her mind: a couple of canoes upended on a grassy stretch near the water with a white truck parked in the background. She had been sure they would see the place, paddling around the canals—and she knew that whoever owned the property would be the person who needed her help.

She sighed. Something was driving her to find that place.

"Hey." Scott's voice carried across the short stretch of water between them, and she heard the swish of his paddle before a spray of water splashed on her bare knee. "Are you sleeping on the job? We've got to paddle back yet."

She smiled, not opening her eyes. "I'm enjoying the serenity. And the tide's doing all the work anyway."

"Maybe so, but you need to pay a *little* bit of attention. Like now, maybe?"

Georgie turned to squint at him, then followed his pointing finger to see the bank a lot closer than she expected. "Oh. Right." She grabbed her paddle and used it to push back from the tangle of tree roots. "Momentary lapse."

They continued, lazily matching stroke for stroke, until finally, Scott said, "So what do you want to do? Keep looking?"

"Let's go back to the jetty at Sussex Inlet," she suggested. "Load the kayaks on the car, have a cup of coffee. See what happens."

"Just wait for your next client to come to you?" he said.

"Something like that," Georgie said, unperturbed. "Never failed in the past."

Two kilometers downstream, Chris Moore stopped tinkering with the motor on his ride-on mower, sighed, and finally gave his son some attention.

"No, Drew," he said. "I'm *not* starting up a Facebook

page, and I'm not doing that Twitter thing. I don't understand Twitter. That's your scene, not mine."

"But Dad, it's easy. You can take photos with your phone and post them on Facebook while you're paddling, and so can your clients. It's a no-stress way to promote the business."

No stress, Chris thought bitterly. For the past eight months, his business had been nothing *but* stress.

Clearly, his face mirrored his thoughts, because Drew sighed and said, "I get it that things are tough right now. But it's a glitch, Dad. Things will pick up again. People around here *know* you. It'll all go away."

Chris grunted, wishing it could be that easy.

"I'll help you. I'll set up everything, so all you have to do is take a photo, press a button and zap! It'll be online."

"Drew." Chris closed his eyes, suddenly feeling the weight of it all pressing down on him, backed up by anger that it had come to this. "It'll take more than a few photos to fix things. And maybe it's time I thought about retiring anyway."

"Retire?" Drew's voice betrayed his shock. "You're not old enough to retire!"

"Fifty-four next month." These days, he felt a lot older than fifty-four. "I'm tired of fighting this. It's time I started enjoying life again."

Drew squatted beside him, concern warring with desperation on his face. "But you were saving for your retirement, so you and Mum didn't have to worry about money. You're not ready yet."

"And the way things are going, I'll be lucky to save another cent. I might as well call it quits."

"You can't!" Drew reached out to him, his hand

closing over his father's forearm. "You *love* what you do. You always told us: *Make a living doing what you love, and you'll never work a day in your life.*"

"Right now, it feels like work," Chris said, giving up on the lawnmower and gathering his tools. "Nothing's gone right since that Burns boy brought drugs into the program. Do you know how many schools I've lost? How many *corporate* clients I've lost? This is the second week without a hint of a customer. Not even a walk-in." He stood up and said in a voice ragged with defeat, "Unless there's a dramatic turnaround, I'm throwing in the towel."

"You *can't*," Drew repeated helplessly, rising to his feet.

Chris shook his head and looked away. He was disappointing his son, he knew, but how much could a man take?

"I agree with Drew," came a calm female voice from behind them. "You can't give in yet, Chris."

He turned to find Allie looking at him, her salt-and-pepper hair tamed into the usual thick braid that fell down her back, her green eyes steady. "Remember those early years when you battled to start it up? We had some hard times, but you were convinced you could do it."

"We were a lot younger, then," he pointed out, beginning to feel outnumbered. "It was hard work, but we knew we could do it. This stuff? It's different. Once the word's got out that you can't be trusted, that *kids* aren't safe in your care, it's all over."

"You know there's no substance to that," Allie said. "Everyone around here knows it, too, and they'll say so. Harrison Burns was out of control. The school principal thinks the same, or he wouldn't have expelled him."

"Tell that to the parents," he said. "Tell it to all the schools that canceled. What I hear is that they've decided to use companies that demonstrate," he made quote marks in the air, "*appropriate duty of care.*"

Allie said nothing for a moment, then she sighed. "Don't do anything rash. Please, Chris. Give it a few more months. And let Drew set up Facebook and Twitter for you. It can't hurt."

"And Instagram," Drew added. "Piece of cake, Dad."

Chris was silent, thinking about the insurance claim that had just come through for the kayaks and trailer stolen the previous month. That was money in the bank, money he and Allie might need. The little bit of money she made from her arts and crafts at the markets certainly wouldn't see them through their retirement. What was the point in buying a bunch of new canoes? He'd only have to sell them at a loss.

"Just until the end of June," Allie begged. "If you still feel the same way then, I promise we'll sit down and work out some alternative."

His wife and son both stared at him, their faces hopeful.

He couldn't say 'no' to them. Chris already knew, in his gut, that it was useless. They were entering a quiet time after Easter, with winter just around the corner. How was he supposed to turn things around in the off-season, with no business coming his way and now petty vandalism to cope with as well?

To him, the outcome was clear. But if it would make Allie and Drew smile again, he could hang on for another few months.

"All right," he said, knowing he sounded ungracious. "I suppose so. End of June, then."

"Yes!" Drew sighed in relief. "I'll get to work on the social media for you right away, Dad."

"Thanks, Chris." Allie moved forward and kissed his cheek, rubbing his back reassuringly. "Why don't we all go in and have a council of war, as we used to when we were beginning? Work out the next step."

He couldn't face it now. "Later. After dinner. I'm going in to meet Frank now, pick up a part for the mower. Need anything?"

"No thanks," Allie said. He caught the quick look that she exchanged with Drew, but pretended he didn't see it. They'd probably guessed there was no mower part to pick up, but they wouldn't argue.

"I might drop over tonight, help you plan," Drew said. "That okay?"

Stifling an impulse to say 'not tonight', Chris nodded. "Sure." He looked at his watch as though time was important. "I'd better go. See you both later."

He fished his keys out of his pocket, climbed into his truck, and drove through the gate, dredging up a smile and a wave.

They watched him go, neither looking happy.

Chris couldn't wait to get out of there.

2

Coming Together

THE MOMENT GEORGIE walked back from the cafe to the parking lot and saw the 4WD parked next to their Land-Cruiser, she knew. Her footsteps slowed, and she nudged Scott. "Scott! That truck."

Scott looked where she was pointing and saw the company logo. "*Moore Canoes and Kayaks?*"

"Yes." Her pulse rate increased a fraction. "Remember what I saw? Canoes upended on grass, near the water somewhere, and there was a white truck. It can't be a coincidence."

"But not necessarily *this* truck. You didn't get a name."

"No." She walked around the truck, taking in the roof racks with cradles and the gear in the back seat. Her certainty grew; that odd feeling of coming home, of arrowing in on what she was meant to know. "It's him, I know it. It's either the owner of this vehicle or somebody close to him."

He leaned against the LandCruiser and grinned at

her. "Well, congrats. You've done it again. I guess we wait for him to come back. And then…?" he trailed off and raised an eyebrow.

"And then the tricky part," Georgie acknowledged with a sigh. "It's easy enough if they are open to this kind of stuff if they know who I am and come to find me, but if I have to go to them…."

"It's like a salesman making a cold call," Scott said. He mimicked her American accent. "Hi, you don't know me, but I'm an eighth-generation gypsy with the Sight, and my crystal ball tells me you're in trouble. Can we talk?"

She laughed ruefully. "Exactly."

"We can start by asking him about kayaks."

"Sounds like a plan."

Scott indicated a seat a short distance from the parking lot, overlooking the water. "Might be a long wait. Want to sit?"

"I've got a better idea." Georgie nodded at the nearby boat hire shed, where they could see a youth cleaning a runabout. "Let's do some regular detecting first. See what we can find out about Moore Canoes and Kayaks before he comes back."

Spending an hour talking to Frank hadn't helped much, Chris had to admit. His old friend seemed to agree with Allie and Drew: *You're having a bad run, that's all. Just put your head down and work through it.*

All very well, Chris thought, as long it wasn't *your* business that had hit the skids.

Morosely, he crossed the road and headed for his car, feeling more like climbing into it and going for a long, long drive than going back home, knowing that Allie was walking on eggshells around him. He paused for a moment, watching a fishing boat motor putter by. He could always take some time out, go back for his kayak and spend a few hours paddling around the basin.

Even that seemed to have lost its appeal for now.

No, he had to go home and talk to Allie and try not to snap at her when she wanted to talk about how they could save the business.

He pressed the button to unlock the door, then looked up when he heard footsteps coming his way. It was a young couple: a woman clad in white cotton shorts and a matching top and a tall fellow in shorts and a T-shirt, his eyes hidden behind dark sunglasses. The man gave him a nod then aimed his key fob at the Land-Cruiser in the next parking bay.

Chris looked at the kayaks lashed to their roof racks. "Been exploring the inlet?"

"Sure have," said the man. "Beautiful area."

The woman smiled at Chris, and he saw her glance at the logo on his truck. "*Moore Canoes and Kayaks.* You must know these waterways like the back of your hand."

"Yes. I guess you could say that."

"I wonder…" She looked at the man with her and then back at Chris. "We're just visiting, down from Huskisson for the day. As you can see," she pointed at their kayaks, "we're doing a bit of paddling. Can we pick your brains for a moment? Oh, I'm Georgie, by the way." She offered a hand, which he shook.

"And I'm Scott," said the man, following suit.

"Nice to meet you," said Chris. "I'm Chris Moore. You want a few tips on where to paddle?"

"If you have the time," said Scott. "We're not holding you up?"

I've got nothing but time, thought Chris. "No, it's fine."

"We spent the morning paddling around the canals, but we'd like to explore St Georges Basin," Georgie said. "Is your business retail, like selling canoes, or do you do guided tours? Because we thought that maybe a guide would be good."

"I've taken people out," Chris said cautiously. He hadn't gone paddling with just one or two people for quite some time, and although these two seemed pleasant enough, he wasn't really in the mood for the casual chit chat that went along with an individually tailored tour. "Usually, I have larger groups, though. Corporate clients or schools."

"You do? Great!" Georgie beamed, not appearing to notice his reluctance. "Can we hire you, then?"

"Well…uh…" There was no good reason for him to say 'no'. And given the state of his bank balance, he would be foolish to refuse. Pushing aside the apathy that made him want to decline, Chris nodded. "I can take you if you want."

Georgie's smile grew wider, and her dark eyes gleamed with pleasure. "That sounds great. When would be a good time?"

"Depends on what you had in mind," he said. "And your experience. We can go for a couple of hours, half a day, or all day."

"Scott's had a fair bit of experience. Me, not so much," she admitted. "But I can manage longer sessions with a break here and there." She turned to her partner. "Scott? What do you think?"

"It's a big area, lots to see. Let's make it a day," he suggested. "Maybe work with the tide and get an early start?"

Oh well, thought Chris. A couple with some experience on the water wouldn't be so bad; he wouldn't have to keep an eye on them every second. On the other hand, since they had their own gear, he couldn't factor in kayak hire, so there wouldn't be a lot of profit. So he'd have to make up for that.

He decided to be upfront. "Since you have your own kayaks, I'll have to charge more to make it worth my while." He named a figure, which he thought was fair, considering. "My wife will provide snacks and lunch."

Scott seemed happy enough with the fee. "Done!" he said, sealing the deal with a firm handshake and an easy grin.

Chris gave a nod down past the boat hire shed. "My place is right on the water; just follow the road around. You'll see a sign out front. We might as well leave from there; you can leave your car in the yard." He took out his phone and tapped on an app to check the tides. "Say seven-thirty?"

"Seven thirty it is."

"Okay. Bring water and a wet bag, sunscreen lotion, any extra snacks, a shady hat…but you probably already know that."

"We will," Georgie assured him. "Well, we'll head on back to Huskisson and see you tomorrow. Nice to meet you, Chris."

They climbed into the LandCruiser and waved at him as they left.

Chris watched them go with mixed feelings. They seemed nice enough. Two people and a day's work as a tour guide wasn't going to save the business, but it would perk Allie up.

Besides, it was money, he reminded himself. Every dollar helped.

3

Confrontation

HALF AN HOUR away at Hyams Beach, in a newly renovated house that now had contemporary angles and dark glass as well as million-dollar views of Jervis Bay, Jesse Burns was in the middle of an argument with his youngest son.

For a boy who had grown up lacking for nothing, the kid was showing no appreciation of everything that had been lavished upon him. Jesse had to concede that Harrison, a boy with plenty of brains and a cunning mind that would have made him a perfect successor to the family business, was a lazy sod.

A lazy sod who had already caused trouble and looked set to cause more. Jesse drummed his fingers on his desk as he stared at Harrison, and his frown deepened.

The boy huffed out an impatient breath. "I can see that you're going to say no." His handsome face darkened, and he stalked over to the window to stare out at the ocean, indignation in every line of his body. Then he whirled around and glared. "I don't need to go back to school to get ahead. *You* know that, Dad. You left school at sixteen, and look at you. You have more money than God."

"I didn't have a choice," his father pointed out. "You do. And things are different these days."

"How? *How* are they different? You figure out how to make money, you do it, and you make *more* money. A stupid degree isn't going to change that." Harrison's dark eyes snapped with fury. "It doesn't make any sense to go back and do Year 12 again at some new school and *then* spend years at university before I can even get started. If you give me a stake, I can be independent in no time."

"Two hundred grand?" It was all Jesse could do not to laugh in his face. "Not going to happen."

Harrison threw his hands up in the air. *"Why?* You can afford it! And I'll pay the damn money back." He flung himself into the chair in front of the desk. "You keep telling me to make something of myself, but when I try, you cut me off at the knees."

"Harrison, you don't have the maturity to start a business."

"Look at Bill Gates. Dick Smith. Mark Zuckerberg. They all started young." His mouth thinned. "You gave money to Nicholas to start *his* business."

Jesse sighed. "Only after insisting your brother spend a substantial amount of time fine-tuning his business plan first. And he was a lot older than you when he started, with a degree in marketing in his pocket." He took a moment to calm himself and linked his fingers over the contracts he had been reading before Harrison burst in. "This is just some harebrained idea you dreamed up in the last week with Tyler Hamilton."

That earned him another glare. *"Harebrained?* Thanks very much, Dad. This is the first thing I've really wanted to do, something I'll work at, and what support do I get? None!"

Jesse had just about had enough. He'd already forked out far too much money to get Harrison out of his hair for a while after the kid got kicked out of White Sands College. He'd given in to his pleas to go back-packing for six months with his friend Tyler and look where that had led.

Endless requests for more money, a SCUBA course, and then an advanced SCUBA course, and now the two of them thought they could set up a business taking people diving in Jervis Bay. Just like that.

The kid didn't have a clue.

Harrison seemed to take his silence for acceptance. "C'mon on, Dad. Let me show you what I can do."

Jesse sighed. "Where's your business plan? Projections for the first three months, six months, first year? How do you plan to promote this? Crew? Staff? First aid training? Insurance? Backup plan?"

"We'll get to all that, all right? Once we know that you're on board, we can get started."

Jesse picked up a pen, twirled it around, and considered what he might say. Since his answer was going to be 'no', Harrison was going to go ballistic anyway. Might as well call a spade a spade.

"Starting a business requires more than money. More than planning, although for me, that's an iron-clad requirement." He held Harrison's gaze. "It requires stamina and, as I've already mentioned, a certain level of maturity." He was silent for a beat and then said, "I might be rich now, but I got that way by being a good judge of character *and* by learning not to invest in a startup with little chance of success. That's why I'm still saying *no*. Drugs and business don't mix, Harrison."

He put the pen down and opened the folder in front of him, signaling that the conversation was over.

As he had expected, Harrison didn't take it well.

"Drugs? *What* drugs?" His son's voice rose. "You're not still on about that business last year? For God's sake, aren't you ever going to let me live that down?"

"I would have," his father said, "if it had been a one-off."

"It *was*."

"I wish that were true."

"What are you talking about?" Harrison bounced to his feet with such force that his chair tipped over. "I don't *touch* drugs anymore. I was a *kid*." His face was red with fury.

"You still are a kid," Jesse pointed out, striving to keep his voice level. "And I can nominate ten different occasions in the past month that you've bought drugs. Much as I hate to say this about my own son, you're a liar and a leech, Harrison." He stood up, so they were at eye level. "And there's no way I'm giving you any money."

"I don't know what you're talking about." Harrison's voice got louder, but his eyes skittered away from his father's. "Someone's been lying. Is it Leah? She's always had it in for me."

"No, it's not your sister. Or your brother." Jesse, sick with disappointment and anger, stared at him. "I hired a private investigator. I have photos, Harrison: times and dates, both here and in Sydney. You have a choice: shape up or ship out." He pointed at the door to emphasize his point. "You've already done enough to ruin my reputation around here. No more, do you hear? *No more.*"

For a moment, he thought his son was going to lunge forward and attack him, but he seemed to have just enough self-control to hold back.

"I was a kid," Harrison spat. "One mistake—*one!*—and I'm kicked out of that shitty outdoor program, kicked out of school. The Principal caved in to the parents; you know he did."

"Harrison, the school had a no-tolerance drug program. He had no choice."

But Harrison was on a roll. "First them, now you. Well, I'll do it without you. I'll show the lot of you, and you'll regret it." He turned, almost fell over the chair he'd upended onto the floor, and kicked it out of the way before striding to the door. There, he turned, his eyes venomous. "You'll be sorry. You'll *all* be sorry."

He slammed the door behind him, and Jesse stood there for a moment, adrenaline making his heart race, before he crossed the room to stare unseeingly at his million-dollar view.

It would be necessary to move swiftly before Harrison spiraled out of control.

4

Pieces of the Puzzle

"Yes, this is the place!" Georgie said with satisfaction as they drove through the gate of *Moore Canoes and Kayaks* the next morning. She pointed at a couple of canoes lying hull-up on the grassy slope leading down to the water, and her gaze swept up to the modest white weatherboard cottage next to a large shed and a shipping container. "This is definitely it. If we'd headed the other way yesterday instead of choosing the canals, we would have seen it from the water."

"Odd that you didn't pick up anything new from your reading last night," Scott said. "After meeting him yesterday, I thought you might."

"I was hoping so too, but that's the way it goes." Georgie had felt frustrated but not surprised. By now, she was used to the way information came to her through her great-grandma Rosa's crystal ball. Sometimes she got a flood of information, sometimes nothing. Sometimes she got clear images, sometimes words, or just a 'knowing' that something was so. It was an annoyingly inexact science, but it was what it was.

Actually, not a science at all, she thought fleetingly as she got out of the car. Reading a crystal ball was all about intuitive leaps and tapping into *something*, but she had never been able to figure out exactly what. She usually thought of it, somewhat ruefully, as *the great unknown*.

Up at the house, a screen door opened, and Chris called to them. "Be with you in a moment!"

"Take your time," Scott called back, waving.

The two of them unstrapped their kayaks and paddles and lowered them to the ground. Georgie slapped on some sun cream and mosquito repellent and then passed it to Scott while she pulled on her rubber kayak shoes.

Chris reached them just as they finished. "All set?"

"Raring to go," Scott said.

Georgie's eyes went to the woman walking down towards them from the house, dressed in a long, floaty caftan and sandals. Chris's wife, she guessed; an assessment confirmed when she reached them.

"My wife Allie," Chris said. "Allie, meet Scott and Georgie."

She smiled at them. "You've got a lovely day for it. Chris was saying you've done some kayaking before?"

Georgie indicated Scott. "He has. I'm less experienced, but I'm learning."

Allie tipped her head to one side when she heard Georgie's accent. "Are you visiting from America?"

"Georgie is," Scott said. "I'm from Queensland, but I worked in the USA for a while. Now I'm showing Georgie some of Australia."

"We're staying at Huskisson," Georgie explained. "We have a trailer there."

"Caravan," Scott said with a grin.

Georgie laughed. "I used to travel around the US in a gypsy caravan," she said. "It sounded right to call it a caravan, given its heritage. But to me, everything else was a trailer. Big modern ones, cute little retro trailers." She glanced at Scott and saw from the quirk at the corner of his lips that he had picked up on her casually dropped reference to gypsies.

Diverted, Allie grinned at her. "A gypsy caravan? I've seen photos of them online. But I think they were all horse-drawn. You didn't have a horse, I'm guessing."

"No," Georgie smiled back, pleased at Allie's interest. "My great-grandma Rosa did, though. She traveled around in a real gypsy caravan, pulled by a horse, and told fortunes with her crystal ball. Mine was a modern-day version, with all mod cons." She heaved a sigh and sent a nostalgic look in Scott's direction. "I lived in it for a year. I have to admit that I miss it."

As she had hoped, Allie ignored her comment about the caravan and homed in on the most interesting fact, edging closer. "Your great-grandmother was a gypsy? With a crystal ball? Really?"

Scott came in right on cue. "She sure was, and Georgie inherited her ability. *And* her crystal ball."

"You're kidding." Allie stared at Georgie and then cast a quick look at her husband. "You can see the future?"

Chris frowned and moved restively, giving his wife a warning look. "Allie's always been into all that stuff. Tarot cards, psychics, runes, you name it."

Gotcha, thought Georgie. In her experience, women usually seemed more interested than men in having fortunes told. Through Allie, they might be able to help

Chris. She gave a casual laugh. "It's not that easy," she responded to Allie. "Sometimes I can see what's going to happen, but often it's in riddles." Subtly, she poked Scott to help carry the conversation.

"She's being modest," he said, giving her ponytail an affectionate tug. "Georgie's helped a lot of people, but she doesn't like to advertise it. Too many charlatans around. So it's mostly for fun now, hey, Georgie?"

"That's right," she agreed, giving Allie a sunny smile and keeping it light. "I'll do a reading for you later if you like. But if I see that you're going to run off with a tall, dark stranger, should I share that with Chris?"

Allie laughed, and Chris gave a strained smile. "Just as long as you see a leggy blonde in my future to compensate. Well, are we ready?" He bent to pick up the rope attached to the nose of his kayak and headed for the water's edge.

"We're looking forward to it," Georgie said. She looked at the water and then up at the perfect blue sky before turning her attention to Allie again. "I'm so glad Chris was available today. We're going to enjoy this. Nothing like having a local guide."

A shadow crossed Allie's face, and she glanced after her husband to make sure he was out of earshot before responding. "He's not had a lot of clients lately, to tell the truth." After a beat, she said in a rush, "Did you mean what you said about a reading? Will you really do that?"

"Of course!" Georgie bent to pick up the nose of her kayak. "Let's line it up when we get back."

"Would you like to stay for dinner when you're done for the day? It'd save you going back and cooking," Allie said in a rush. Then she made a face and added, "Only you want to. No pressure. Sorry, I'm being pushy. I guess your crystal ball is back in your caravan anyway."

It would have been, thought Georgie, if she hadn't been hoping that they could talk Chris into a reading today. She hid a smile. "It's in the car. So we can do it today if you want. But we don't want to impose on you for dinner."

"Nonsense. We have to eat anyway; I'll just throw in a bit extra." Allie looked excited—and hopeful.

For a moment, Georgie felt uneasy. If she got as little as she had the night before from the crystal ball, Allie would be disappointed.

No, she couldn't think like that. She had been drawn to this little canoe business at Sussex Inlet for a reason. Her crystal ball wouldn't let her down.

Down at the water's edge, Scott and Chris were looking back, waiting for her.

"I'm coming!" she called and then looked back at Allie. "Thanks, dinner would be lovely. See you later!"

Allie's eyes met hers. "Thank you." She looked as though she wanted to say more but contented herself with a small smile. "Later." She waved and walked back to the house.

***

Allie watched from the window as the three kayaks disappeared around the bend, heading for the Basin. For the first time in months, she felt hope. It had to mean something, a genuine gypsy fortune-teller turning up on her doorstep like this.

She already knew from his comments when Georgie was talking about her great-grandma's crystal ball that Chris was wary—probably thinking, *Oh please, not a gypsy fortune teller. It'll only make things worse.*

Of course, things could go the other way. Instead of seeing things turning around for them, getting better, Georgie might see complete disaster. Would she tell them if the news wasn't good?

Maybe she wouldn't. Perhaps she would just gloss over it somehow, talk in generalities, or tell them other stuff that didn't matter.

Allie frowned. She'd try to have a word to Georgie first, when Chris wasn't around, and tell her that she wanted the truth, whatever it might be.

She turned away from the window and went back to the small desk in the corner of the family room, and opened the blue folder there labeled *Bills, Payable*. She fanned through them, sighing. When she closed the laptop computer the night before, she had felt sick at the thought of how little they had to carry them through. She'd been wondering if she could spend more hours making her jewelry and the caftans that were so popular with tourists and going further afield in search of more weekend markets. But in her heart of hearts, she knew that it wouldn't be enough.

They'd have to face facts. If there was no way to keep the business going, then they'd just have to look things squarely in the face and make hard choices.

But no matter what Chris said, she refused to believe that the business they'd worked so hard on couldn't be built up again. The theft of the canoes a few weeks ago had probably been the straw that broke the camel's back. After months of watching the business go downhill, after the pain of having his good reputation destroyed, being targeted by thieves was just too much.

Chris deserved better. They *both* deserved better.

All she wanted from Georgie was a sign that they should hang on. Just a tiny ray of hope.

5

Revelations

CHRIS MOORE really did love his work, Georgie thought, watching him paddling along just ahead of her. She could see it: his enjoyment of the outdoors, his at-one-ness with the water and the wildlife. His mouth had lost some of the tightness she had seen earlier.

She didn't yet know his story, but already, she wanted to help Chris and Allie. She felt for them, two hard-working people who had built up a business only to watch it fail.

They'd found out a little from chatting to Ross at the boat hire shed, who had been more than happy to talk about his town as he worked. She and Scott hadn't charged right in with questions about *Moore Canoes and Kayaks*, of course. They'd talked about how nice the area was and what they'd been doing at Huskisson, and then led up to what they wanted to know by telling him where they'd been that morning. They finished with a casual query about the truck in the parking lot: "We saw the truck over there. Is there a canoe and kayak shop in town?"

He told them it was not a sales outlet but a business that mostly took out groups from schools. He liked the owner; it seemed: *"Good bloke, Chris Moore. He'll see you right, pity things have been so quiet for him lately—a bit of a downturn."* He hadn't elaborated, launching immediately into a discussion about his own business and suggesting that they hire a motorboat to go up and explore Basin View and Sanctuary Point.

Exactly what 'a bit of a downturn' meant for Chris Moore, she wasn't sure, but instinct told her that there was a lot more behind it than Ross-from-boat-hire suggested.

Today, she should be able to find out more.

After an hour or so, they stopped at a tiny sandy beach on the shore for a break, and she finally got a chance to talk with Chris.

She and Scott kept it light, chatting about some of their travels in the States before leading the conversation to Georgie's father's RV empire and telling their guide how he built modern-day versions of retro trailers and gypsy caravans.

Georgie changed the subject, without mentioning the crystal ball again, when she saw a hint of wariness in his eyes at the mention of gypsy caravans. No need to spook him.

"Enough about us, Chris," she said with a smile. "I want to learn all I can about Australia and its people. What about you, your family? Have you always lived around here?"

He nodded. "Dad's a mechanic, retired now, but still works on cars for people around here. My two sisters have moved away, but I've always loved it here. Jervis Bay, St Georges Basin—I'd never leave."

"I can see why," Georgie said warmly, with a glance around at their surroundings. "How old were you when you started your business?"

Chris stared into the distance, a faraway look in his eyes. "I'd just turned twenty-six when Allie and I registered the company. Before that, I worked for my grandfather as a mechanic, but I'd go away every chance I'd get, most weekends…always hiking, boats, water. I worked for an outdoor adventure company that took school groups away, and I thought, *I could do that for myself.* When I married Allie, she was keen to start our own business, so… we did. We had two babies, Drew and Katie, and we were poor, so it was a battle at times. But, we did it."

Watching him, Georgie saw that the pinched look had come back to his face. When she glanced at Scott, she caught him staring thoughtfully at Chris before he shot a quick look at her, giving a barely noticeable nod.

"I always like to hear about people taking things into their own hands, doing what they love," she said. "It must be very rewarding for you."

Chris said nothing for a moment but then met her gaze. "It used to be. Things haven't been going so well lately." He shrugged and injected a note of false cheer in his voice, screwing up a sandwich wrapper and putting it in his pocket to dispose of later. "It'll pick up, I guess. Ready to move on?"

"I might take just ten minutes more if that's okay," Georgie said, stretching her legs out in front of her. "We did quite a bit yesterday." She grinned at Scott. "I'm not as fit as some."

"I'll have to send you to boot camp," Scott said. "Toughen up a bit." He leaned back against a rock, turning his face up to the sun, and said casually, "If I might ask… why *haven't* things been going well, Chris? Is it always quiet at this time of year?"

He nodded. "After Easter, business always slackens off. School groups tend to pick the warmer months for outdoor camps and such. But I…" Chris sighed, and after another short pause, said, "There was a bit of an incident eight months ago, and there have been… repercussions."

Georgie pushed him a little further. "Oh, I'm sorry to hear that. If I'm not being too nosy… what happened?"

For a moment, he said nothing, then he shrugged. "Everyone else around here knows, so I can't see that it matters if you do, too."

They waited, both of them watching Chris.

"School group," he finally said. "There's this swanky private college here, White Sands College. You wouldn't have heard of it. It's on a par with some of the Sydney private schools, but smaller. A bit elitist."

Georgie looked at Scott and raised her eyebrows in a query.

"No," he said. "Haven't heard of it."

"Thought not," Chris said. "They have a secondary campus down the coast a bit, a place where they do outdoor activities. A dozen cabins, high and low ropes, abseiling, hiking, biking, kayaking. They hire different outdoor companies to take the kids. I got the contract for kayaking. Sometimes I take staff groups as well, but it's mostly kids."

They nodded.

"To cut a long story short," he said, "We had this group of Year 12 kids there. It was their last outdoor camp before the final exams. I had two of my most experienced staff in charge of the group. Everything was going well until one of the stragglers ran into trouble." He glanced at them. "They were two-person canoes, so we had two kids in each one."

"Right," said Scott.

"One canoe tipped over, and the kids in it panicked a bit, so both group leaders went back to help. They told the others to wait until we were all ready to go again, but two of the boys sneaked ahead." He picked up a nearby pebble and hurled it into the water, his jaw working. "A couple of others followed them and saw what happened. One boy stood up and started horsing around, rocking it to scare the other kid. Inevitably, it turned over too, but this time one of the boys got trapped underneath. My staff got there just in time."

"Oh. How terrible." Georgie hadn't expected anything this serious. "Was he… all right?"

"He was, thanks to their training. But there was an inquiry, and they found that Harrison Burns—the idiot who was horsing around—had brought drugs with him to the camp, and he and a few of the others were high."

Whoa, trouble, thought Georgie. After a short silence, she asked, "And they blamed you?"

"Not formally, no. But the school had recently embarked on a zero-tolerance program for drugs, so Harrison and two of the others were expelled. Their father is a big wheel at the school, donates lots of money, and isn't happy. He made noises, but they refused to allow Harrison to stay until final exams. Meanwhile, my contract was terminated."

Georgie kept her eyes on him, sensing there was

more to come. Just one school contract couldn't make this much difference to a business.

Sounding weary, Chris went on. "Over the next few months, other schools found different providers. Then the corporate groups dried up. You can imagine what it's like: once the word is out that someone in charge of kids allows drugs into the group, no one wants to take the risk. It was Harrison Burns that brought them in, but rumors circulated about my staff dealing drugs. Nobody ever said anything directly, even when I pushed them. They all had other reasons for not being able to use me anymore, but I knew."

"I'm so sorry," Georgie said. "That's tough when none of it was your fault."

"Then," he said, "Last month, a few days before I was due to take away a small group from a business up north, some piece of trash stole my trailer loaded with canoes. They found it dumped in the scrub a few miles up the road, with all the canoes wrecked. To continue with the program, I had to hire replacements from someone else. So, profits were down on that one." He looked up and forced a smile. "It's getting so I don't know whether I *want* to keep going, to be honest. It was good while it lasted, but maybe my time is over."

"Sorry to hear that, mate," Scott said. "You've had a bad run, all right. You don't think it will all blow over?"

"It's more competitive out there now. I'd need someone to go in to bat for me, and there isn't anyone. I'm just a small town bloke with a small town business. There are plenty queuing up to fill my shoes." He stood up and stretched. "My problem is convincing Allie that it's time to move on. She wants to keep fighting." He extended a hand to Georgie. "Recovered enough to keep going?" His tone made it clear that the discussion was over.

"You're in league with Scott," she said, pretending to be aggrieved as she let him haul her to her feet. "Determined to make me suffer. Okay, okay. But I'm riding the current *all* the way back."

The men both laughed, and they put back into the water.

Georgie, paddling along a little behind them, thought about what she'd heard.

Was Chris's bad luck a result of just one unlucky incident that sent things spiraling down, or was there more to it?

More, the voice in her head said firmly. *You're here, aren't you?*

6

First Reading

WHEN THEY ROUNDED the bend at around five at Chris's place, Allie was waiting for them, lolling back in a camp chair with a book in her hands. When she spotted them, she sat up and waved.

Georgie envied her the deck chair. After a whole day's kayaking, every muscle was sore. To think that Scott had done this for ten days, paddling along the Missouri! He was made of sterner stuff than she. She stretched and let out a small groan.

Scott grinned at her. "Had enough?"

"For about the next month," she said ruefully. "But it was fun."

Scott hung back with Georgie and let Chris beach his kayak first. "Does he know we're staying for dinner?" he said in a low voice.

"I forgot to mention it once he started talking about his problems," Georgie murmured back. "Well, he can hardly un-invite us, can he?" With a few fast strokes, she sent her kayak in after Chris, grinning at Allie. "Hi!

Sorry, I think we're a bit later than we thought. At least we worked up an appetite."

"It's just lasagne and salad," Allie said. "But plenty of it. I'll go and make coffee while you get yourselves organized here."

Out of the corner of her eye, Georgie saw Chris's head whip around towards his wife. He said nothing, but she could imagine the look he had sent her.

Allie smiled at her husband, looking unperturbed. "Did Georgie tell you I asked them to stay for dinner? I'm dying to hear more about her travels."

"No," Chris said brusquely, "but they're more than welcome." He hauled his kayak higher up the grassy slope and flipped it over to drain, without looking at Scott or Georgie.

"Chris has already heard a few stories," Georgie said cheerfully. "We'll have to come up with some different ones for you."

"Maybe Jerry and the Preppers," Scott suggested. "That's a good one."

That made Chris turn and look at them, arching an eyebrow. "Jerry and the Preppers? Sounds like a pop group."

"Jerry's my brother," Georgie told him. "Remember we told you about my father's RV business? Well, Jerry had a sideline in making bug-out vehicles for preppers—you know, survivalists, preparing for Doomsday. The problem was that he got involved with a couple of hard-core crazies. They kidnapped him."

"*Kidnapped* him?" Chris looked reluctantly intrigued. "I have to admit *that* sounds like a tale that needs telling."

"You've no idea," Georgie said, laughing as she tugged off her kayak booties. "We've got enough stories to keep you up until midnight."

And, she thought with satisfaction, a few of them should make Chris more receptive to the idea of a crystal ball reading.

Then they might have some idea where all of this was heading.

Almost an hour later, when she judged that Chris had become accustomed to the idea that there might be more to a crystal ball than a gimmick at a sideshow, Georgie managed to catch Allie's eye. She gave a slight nod towards Chris, talking with Scott about his kayaking experiences along the Missouri.

Allie nodded back, and Georgie drained her coffee cup before saying, "So, Allie…would you still like me to do a reading, or have we put you off with all these stories?"

"Hardly," Allie responded. "Quite the opposite." She sent a bright smile across the table at her husband. "We wouldn't turn this down, would we, Chris?"

"*You* wouldn't," he said wryly. "You've never walked past a tarot reader at the markets in your life."

Georgie stood up. "My crystal ball is in the car." She winked at Chris, gesturing down at her shorts and cotton sleeveless top. "I don't have my great-gran's genuine gypsy shawl with me, or I'd dress up for you. I'm sure it would make me look more authentic."

"Actually," Allie said, "the tarot reader who comes to

our local market looks like she should be selling cakes for a school fund-raiser. She just has a fold-up table under a pop-up gazebo."

"And Allie still believes everything she says," Chris said. "So you should be fine." Looking resigned, he stood up. "I'll clear the table."

"I'll help," said Scott. He clapped Chris on the shoulder. "Don't worry; it'll be relatively painless. No smoke and mirrors."

That made Chris grin. "It's one way to pass the evening."

Good, thought Georgie. At least she wasn't going to be sitting down with a totally reluctant subject.

Now all she had to do was come up with the goods.

They sat at a round table, with Allie and Chris on either side of Georgie. Allie edged forward in her seat to peer at the crystal ball. Chris had his arms folded and a neutral expression on his face. He was being polite, Georgie guessed, although she thought he might have warmed up a little after hearing about a few of her successes.

As though he were reading her mind, he said suddenly, "So you use this crystal ball to solve crimes?"

"It has worked out that way," Georgie admitted. "In the beginning, our little crystal ball investigation team was more of a joke, but we all worked well together. Layla was great with a computer and research, and Tammy—well, how can I describe Tammy?"

"Your brother's fiancée," Allie said, showing she'd

been listening. "The girl who looks like Doris Day and shoots like Annie Oakley."

Georgie and Scott looked at each other and laughed. "Close enough," said Georgie.

"You must miss them."

"You don't know how much," Georgie said feelingly. "But out here, we have Scott's mother, who is into astrology and reads cards. And Scott's no slouch himself, of course."

Allie looked at him, open-mouthed. "What do you do?"

"I read cards a little," he said easily. "Couldn't help but pick it up from Ma."

"He's being modest," Georgie told Allie. "He's quite good, and the more he does it, the better he gets. And then there's his brother, Bluey."

"He reads cards too?" Chris shook his head. "This sounds like a TV show. Kind of X Files meets CSI."

"No, Bluey's never gone in for that kind of thing," Scott said. "He...uh...he's pretty good with computers and research too, like Layla was back in the States. He looks up stuff for us." He sent Georgie a bland look, and she grinned at him. They couldn't tell most people that Scott's brother hacked into online places where he wasn't supposed to be. Not that he had ever admitted it.

"Okay," she said. "Time to get this show on the road."

Allie looked around. "Do you need the curtains drawn or anything?"

"No," Georgie said. "I often use a candle as a focal point, but it's not necessary." She glanced from Allie to Chris. "Is there anything, in particular, you want to know?"

The two of them spoke at the same time.

"Yes," Allie said.

"No," said her husband.

"We *do*, Chris," Allie said. "We want to know how things are going to work out for us. And I don't know about you, but…" her forehead creased, "but *I'd* like to know who trashed our canoes."

"Fine," Chris said, his voice somewhat testy. "Should we ask Georgie to provide us with a full description, address, and phone number?"

"Don't hold your breath," Georgie said with a smile. "I have to warn you; this could be a complete disappointment. I've had readings where I've got zilch and others where I've seen a face clearly or heard a name. Sorry, but no guarantees."

Allie looked embarrassed. "I didn't mean to put pressure on you."

"You didn't," Georgie said firmly, patting her on the hand. "What I'm going to do is just be open to whatever comes, right? If you have a question, just hold it in your mind. We'll see what happens."

From the other side of the table, Scott gave her a nod and a small smile, and Georgie relaxed, appreciating the tacit support as she focused on the globe in front of her.

At first, she could see only her reflection and light reflected from the setting sun coming through the window, but as she shut out the world around her, the first tendrils of mist formed in the center of the crystal ball. These days, she shifted fairly easily into what she thought of as 'the zone'. A place that was here, yet not here; a place where information could flow to her unimpeded by the subtle noise of the everyday world.

A far cry, she thought fleetingly, from her first experience with a crystal ball, when she had been completely inexperienced and a little scared of it all.

The mist thickened, and then gradually, the wisps parted to show a scene. Georgie frowned at it, not sure at first what she was seeing.

Two figures, one a boy in a school uniform, the other a man wearing a yellow polo shirt and shorts. She could see the face of the boy, but the man had his back turned. Both were a bit fuzzy. It didn't help that the one in the yellow polo shirt was wearing a soft cotton hat with a floppy brim. From the angry gestures, it was clear they were arguing, and then the man in yellow passed something to the boy.

She closed her eyes for a fraction of a second, concentrating on being open for other information—a name, a feeling, a tiny flash of understanding.

A picture appeared in her mind, just for a second. A logo… the one she'd seen on Chris Moore's vehicle. A simple silhouette of a person in a canoe, paddle raised, with waves stitched underneath it.

With waves *stitched* underneath it?

Oh. She was seeing the logo as it would look on a shirt, not painted on a car.

So this transaction, whatever it was…this *argument*, had something to do with Chris's business, *Moore Canoes and Kayaks?*

Looking back at the image in the crystal ball, she homed in on the schoolboy. It was like looking at a photo slightly out of focus, but she stared at him until she was sure she'd remember the face: a square jaw, a dark sweep of hair across the boy's forehead, winged eyebrows.

He moved, and she caught a glint of light at his ear.

An earring or a stud no, wait: it was a disc. He had one of those things that some youths inserted into an earlobe, stretching it. That might be a useful snippet of information.

Then the male in the yellow polo shirt moved but still didn't turn so that she could see his face. It was as though she was behind them and looking down slightly. A floppy hat, a yellow shirt—it wasn't much to go on. Frustrated, Georgie wished—not for the first time—that she could slip inside the crystal ball and walk around in the scene; take a really good look.

But it didn't work that way. She saw what she saw, for good or bad.

"Omigod." Allie's voice sounded awed. "You really *can* see things in it. I mean, *I* can see… I didn't think that I'd be able to…."

Glancing up, Georgie saw her with a hand to her mouth, her gaze fixed on the figures in the crystal ball.

"Some people can; some can't," she said. "What do you see?"

"A boy. A man. I'm sure…." Allie's eyes left the crystal ball, and she turned to look at her husband, sitting next to her. "I'd swear the boy is Harrison Burns. Can you see them, Chris?"

He was frozen, staring at the tiny figures in the crystal ball. His arms were still folded, but his fingers were digging into his skin.

"Chris?"

"Yes." Finally, he looked at her. "It's small and not that clear, but it looks like him. But the other one…."

Allie seemed to know what he was thinking without

being told. She closed her eyes and took a deep breath. "The other one. He's wearing one of our company t-shirts. Whoever Harrison is talking to; he's one of ours. Chris, does this mean…."

"Does this mean," Chris finished for her, his brows coming together in an angry slash, "that one of our *staff* gave him those drugs?"

He and Allie stared at each other for a moment. Allie's gaze returned to the crystal ball, and she frowned. "I wish we could see his face. How much do you want to bet it's Jason Hoy?"

"It's got to be," Chris said grimly. "The other guys have been working for me for years."

"Jason Hoy…?" Georgie raised an eyebrow.

"Lazy," Chris said. "Inclined to take shortcuts with safety and supervision. I had to let him go not long after that incident with Harrison. He wasn't one of the supervisors on that day, thank goodness."

Jason Hoy. Georgie felt the familiar tiny curl of excitement that meant she had found a thread to tug on.

Whether Jason Hoy had been the one to provide Harrison with drugs or not, that name resonated in her mind. She needed to see him, as long as he hadn't moved to the other side of the country. "Where did he go after he left?"

"He worked for a canoe hire place in Huskisson for a while, but he got the boot from there too," Chris said. "I don't know where he is now."

"I do," Allie said.

Every eye turned to her.

"He's a casual at the Pub'n'Grub," she said.

"Annette at the Book Club told me. She said she had a meal there last week, and she didn't plan to go back any time soon. Awful food, and the bar service was terrible. Guess who was working behind the bar?"

7

Tugging at Threads

"THAT'S HIM," Georgie murmured as they walked into the Riverside Pub'n'Grub. She recognized Jason Hoy immediately from a photo Chris had shown them, although he seemed thinner. Looking bored, he was stacking a wire shelf with packets of potato chips. The black t-shirt with the pub logo hung loosely over jeans that badly needed a wash. So did his hair, carelessly brushed back from his face and tucked behind his ears.

Scott eyed the blackboard menu dubiously. "We're not eating here, are we?"

"Not after what Allie's friend had to say about it. We'll see if we can get him to talk, then go somewhere else for lunch."

They perched on a couple of stools at the bar, waiting for him to acknowledge them.

Jason glanced at them briefly and then took the empty carton into a back room before finally coming their way. He raised his eyebrows. "Help you?"

"Lemon, lime, and bitters, thanks," Georgie said. "Easy on the bitters."

"Same for me," Scott echoed. "Normal shot of bitters."

Their target plucked a couple of glasses from a rack and added ice before reaching for the bitters.

"Nice town," Georgie ventured.

"You think?" he said with disinterest. "I s'pose it's all right to visit." Without looking at them, he took his time making the drinks and then rang up the sale. "Nine dollars, thanks."

"You don't sound all that keen on the area," Scott said, handing over the money.

"You ought to try living here. Town's dead." Jason plucked a dollar in change out of the till and held it out, right over the tips jar. "There you go."

"Thanks." Smiling at him, Georgie took it from him and dropped it in the jar with the small change that barely covered the bottom. It would be worth a dollar to get him to talk. "I'm Georgie. And you?"

"Jason." He started to move away but stopped when she spoke swiftly to keep him there.

"Are you a local, Jason?"

"No. Been here a year or so."

"Oh, not that long, then." She took a sip and smiled at him. "What brought you here in the first place?"

"Came down for the weekend with a mate," he said. "Heard there was a job going, so I applied for it and stayed."

A year ago, Georgie thought. Probably the job with Chris. The time frame sounded about right, if Chris had given him a fair chance to prove himself before letting him go.

Pretending ignorance, she said, "So you've been working here in the hotel for a year?"

"No." He took a step away from them and picked up a damp cloth to wipe over the counter. "Worked with a canoe place for a while, taking out school kids."

"That must have had its moments. Kids can be a challenge." Georgie beamed at him. "We were out on the water in our kayaks yesterday with a guy named Chris Moore. He said he does stuff with schools. Was that who you worked for?"

That got his attention. Finally, he looked at her. "Yeah, that was the one."

"Chris said it's getting towards the low season now." She sipped her drink and then held it up, arching her eyebrows in a query. "Is that why you decided to switch to doing this? Not enough work with the canoe place?"

"One of the reasons. Moore isn't the easiest bloke to work for."

"Oh?" She opened her eyes wide and then looked thoughtful. "I must admit, he didn't talk much, did he, Scott?"

"Man of a few words," Scott acknowledged. "A hard taskmaster, was he?"

Jason sneered. "An old woman, more like. Treated those kids like they were five-year-olds instead of Year 12. Do this, do that, wait for me, follow the instructions."

"And treated his staff the same way, maybe?" Scott prompted.

"You got it." Scenting a sympathetic audience, Jason put down the cloth and came closer, leaning his elbows on the counter. "Me, I think you gotta give kids a bit of credit for having some common sense."

"Some of them," Georgie acknowledged. "High school kids, though… they can be hard to handle."

"Yeah, well, I never had any problems," Jason said scornfully. "Kids liked me because I treated them like grownups." He leaned forward confidentially, looking from one of them to the other. "I bet he didn't tell you about the accident, did he?"

"Accident?" Scott put down his drink and mirrored Jason's actions, leaning forward. Dropping his voice a little, he said, "What accident?"

"Couple of kids capsized, got into trouble. Nearly drowned. It came out that they'd been taking drugs. Now, if *I'd* been in charge that day, I would have recognized the signs, had a talk to them, and headed trouble off before it built up."

"So you weren't working that day?" Georgie didn't glance at Scott, but she knew he'd be thinking the same as she was: if Jason Hoy hadn't been there, then he probably wasn't the one in the crystal ball."

"Not on the water. I just drove the mini-bus. Dropped off the kids and left again."

Georgie relaxed. It still could have been Jason she'd seen, then. She went back to his other comment. "What do you mean you'd have recognized the signs? Unless someone was completely off their heads, I don't think I'd be able to tell."

He shrugged. "Their eyes, the way they talk. I can tell by looking at them, mostly."

"Wow." She cast around for a way to keep him talking. "That couldn't have been good for business, kids bringing in drugs with them."

She saw a flicker of wariness in his eyes. "You're right about that." He looked away from her, busying himself with wiping the counter again, and then added, "Some people around here got to wondering about

Moore himself, whether he's making money on the side, just pretending to be strict."

Georgie had to grit her teeth at that one but kept her face bland.

"Seems a bit harsh to put it all on the owner," Scott commented. "He seemed like a decent bloke. Hasn't he been running that business for years?"

"Makes no difference. Supply a few drugs; it's easy money." A tick too late, he added, "So they tell me." Glancing over their shoulders, he suddenly appeared nervous, as if worried that he might have said too much, and started to edge away.

At the other end of the bar, a scruffy guy in his twenties pulled up a stool. Jason Hoy looked his way and nodded as the other man held up one finger. "G'day, Simmo. The usual?"

The other man gave him a thumbs-up and turned his attention to his phone, and Jason picked up a schooner glass and moved away from them.

Scott looked at her and said in an undertone, "He knows something."

"Yes." Georgie drew circles around the rim of her glass, thinking. "But even if we found out for sure that he was the one to bring the drugs into the program, how would that help Chris? Unless..." She checked again that Jason wasn't close enough to overhear them. "Unless Jason himself was helping to spread the rumors that Chris was supplying kids. Revenge for getting sacked?"

"One thing wrong with that scenario. If it's so easy to make money through drugs, why would he bother taking on work as a canoe instructor?"

"Constant contact with buyers?" Georgie tapped her

fingers, thinking. "And following that train of thought, why is he working here in the pub?"

"Same reason," Scott said. "Everyone knows where to find him—and his wares."

They watched Jason set a foaming beer down in front of the guy who'd just come in, leaning forward at the same time to say something in a low voice. He glanced around, then back at them, and narrowed his eyes when he saw where their attention was focused.

Scott pretended he'd been waiting to catch his eye and gave him a wave. "When you've finished there, could you bring us a packet of chips?"

He relaxed and nodded. "Yeah, be there in a minute."

"I just want to get out of here," Georgie mumbled, pushing away her drink. "But we haven't got anything. I need a lead."

"You could try asking him if he'd like his fortune told."

"Hah hah."

Jason finished his conversation with the other man and came back their way with a packet of chips. "Here you go. Three fifty."

"Thanks." Scott handed over a five waved away the change. "Keep it. Use it towards a ticket out of here." He winked at Jason and then said, "What about your friend—the one you came to visit? Did he leave too?"

"Nah. I'm staying with him."

"Does he still work with the canoe guy?" Scott tore open the chip packet and offered it to Georgie.

"Nope," Jason said. "He's a personal trainer. Not much other work around here, unless you're into boats or fishing."

"Well, good luck." As though he had already lost interest in the barman, Scott said to Georgie, "Let's walk and get some fresh air. Maybe have a meal later."

"Good idea." She helped herself to another chip and gave Jason a cursory wave. "Nice meeting you, Jason. Got a long shift today, or will you be able to escape soon?"

He glanced at his watch. "Couple more hours and I'm outta here."

"Enjoy. See you later."

Chad Royston, sitting in a dim booth, had witnessed the whole exchange.

He ate another mouthful of the indifferent lunch in front of him and scowled. A great believer that prevention was better than a cure when it came to being caught handling drugs, he liked to go to the pub from time to time to keep a finger on the pulse of the community.

And to keep an eye on Jason Hoy. He preferred to slip in unseen, if he could, and observe Jason before he was aware that his housemate was there.

He had no great confidence in Jason. He was a bit player—useful enough now he was working at the pub, but someone disposable if he got too big for his boots. He liked to run his mouth a bit too much for Chad's taste—just as he had been over the past fifteen minutes.

Word had trickled down from Sydney that the cops had linked the supply of drugs on the south coast with certain people in the city. It was not welcome news: Chad had been careful, here in Sussex Inlet, to stay one step removed from the action. After the local scandal with Harrison Burns and the incident on the water, he'd been even more paranoid. Sure, there were locals who at least suspected his real role—mostly because they knew others who had bought drugs from him in the past—but these days, he was playing a convincing role as a half-way-decent personal trainer. He was building a reputation as someone who did not recommend steroids or performance-enhancing drugs, even while he surreptitiously provided them to people who could keep their mouths shut.

The couple who had just left had set his "cop" radar on the alert. They were dressed like tourists, but they were asking too many questions for his liking. When they'd struck up a conversation with Jason, he had strained his ears to hear, and the snatches of conversation he'd caught worried him.

Why would they be interested in how long a bartender had been in Sussex Inlet? While he'd been listening to their conversation, Chad had diligently worked his way through the tough steak on his plate, chewing slowly and pretending to be absorbed in the local newspaper folded on his table.

At one point, he'd caught Chris Moore's name. He'd sneaked a glance over at the bar and had seen Jason leaning forward with his elbows on the bar, murmuring about something else. Chad closed his eyes and concentrated on the drift of conversation and had almost choked on the steak he was chewing when he heard 'drugs'.

Drugs. For God's sake, was the idiot honestly telling them about drugs in the school program? Did he *want* a one-way ticket to prison? Chad had closed his eyes briefly, gritting his teeth, and then opened them again to see what he could read from the faces of the two "tourists" at the bar. He sat up straighter in his seat and leaned forward until he managed to catch Jason's eye. Glaring at him, he slashed a finger across his throat in a silent warning. *Stop talking, you moron.*

Jason had hastily glanced away from him, handed the two their change, and mooched off to the end of the bar where one of his regular customers was waiting. There, he leaned forward and had a whispered conversation, pausing for a moment to look back at the tourists. Chad had followed his gaze. Yes, they *were* watching him. The bloke called out and asked Jason for a packet of chips.

When he brought them, the two of them had exchanged a few more sentences that he couldn't catch and then got up off their seats and left.

Now, having heard enough—*more* than enough— Chad pushed aside the plate of food. His fridge at home was packed with much better stuff; he would eat there. And he would have a stern word to Jason Hoy at the earliest opportunity.

———

Scott looked at Georgie quizzically as he held the door open for her. "*Are* you planning on seeing Jason later?"

"Sort of," she said. "I'm planning to follow him. Find out where he lives and see who this friend of his is."

"To what end?"

"Who knows?" she said cheerfully, glad to be outside the hotel at last. "It'll lead somewhere."

Scott sighed. "Spoken like a true gypsy fortune-teller. Knowledge will flow in from the great unknown. Wouldn't it be easier to call Chris and just ask him who recommended Jason?"

Georgie stopped and put her hands on her hips. "Yeah, but that's no fun."

"And…?"

"And because I need to *see* this other guy. Then I can make more sense of what I see in the crystal ball. Okay?"

Scott grinned at her. "If you say so."

"And then," Georgie went on, "after I've had a chance to look at him, we're going to give his name and Jason Hoy's name to your brother and get him to use his super-hacker skills to find out more about them."

"Bluey's not a hacker," Scott said blandly, his eyes dancing.

"So he says. But whatever his real job is, he can find out stuff quicker than we can."

What she wasn't telling Scott was that she was feeling uneasy about the whole thing, as though what happened in the past wasn't going to *stay* in the past.

Chris Moore might have a lot more to worry about than his business slowing down.

8

Reprisals

HARRISON BURNS WAS mad at the world.

As if his father's crappy attitude hadn't been enough, now his *supposed* friend Tyler was smirking at him as though he was some total idiot.

"I knew all along that your old man wouldn't give you the money," he said.

"What do you mean?" Harrison demanded, his blood doing a slow boil. "That's not what you said a few days ago."

Tyler, half out of it on whatever he'd just sniffed or swallowed, squinted at him. "He was never going to give you that kind of cash. He thinks you're a loser." He flopped a leg over the arm of the sofa and closed his eyes. "If it makes you feel any better, my father said 'no' too."

Harrison glared at him, a wasted effort since Tyler wasn't even looking. Testing his friend's capacity to think straight, he said, "So what do we do now?"

"Think of something else." Tyler's voice was slurred.

"We've got to get money from *somewhere*." Harrison seized Tyler's foot and tugged. "Come on, this is important."

Tyler's eyes snapped open, and his voice turned ugly. "Back *off*. And what's this '*we*' business? You're the one who needs money, not me."

Harrison held up both hands in a placatory gesture. While they were backpacking, he had learned the hard way that Tyler was capable of turning feral in a nanosecond. "Jeez, Tyler! All *right!*"

Tyler rolled over on the sofa to shut out the world. "Leave me alone."

Kicking a footstool out of the way, Harrison slammed out of the messy studio apartment under the Hamilton house. He slid behind the wheel of his mother's Prius, a car she drove to prove to the other mothers at the school she cared about the environment. Harrison didn't give a stuff about the environment, but he needed wheels, and the Prius was the only car he was allowed to drive. He'd borrowed it without asking the day before when he'd stormed out of the house, and this morning he'd woken up on Tyler's hard-as-a-rock futon to find his phone full of irate messages from his mother ordering him to bring it back *at once*.

She'd have to wait. He needed wheels. He needed to *think*.

Harrison sat for a moment, thinking, getting angrier and angrier as he tried to find a pathway out of his predicament.

He needed money, and fast, to pay for the drugs he'd used in the past week as well as more to keep him going. So far, he'd been careful about what he took from the house to turn into cash, but his mother was already making waves about her missing necklace with that stupid giant butterfly studded with diamonds: a thing that had been handed down through the family. She'd had a huge bust-up with his sister Leah over it because Leah was always borrowing her stuff and misplacing it, so the two still weren't speaking, even four weeks later.

He couldn't risk stealing any more jewelry. Especially not now that his father was getting more suspicious. It had been hard enough to get rid of the damned pendant—in the end, he'd agreed to leave it in Tyler's hands, when he insisted he could swap it for some good shit, but Harrison believed he'd been played for a sucker over that one. It should have brought in more than the paltry supplies Tyler brought back. According to his mother, the thing was worth about sixty grand.

Now, Harrison owed nearly four grand to one of his suppliers and another grand to Tyler, and Tyler was asking for his money back because *he* had to pay someone.

What a mess.

He rested his head on the steering wheel and tried to order his thoughts.

No loan from his father.

No money from Tyler.

No drugs for tonight, and he couldn't get any more until he paid up.

Everything had been going along just fine, he thought resentfully, until he got kicked out of school. His father, the principal, the canoe guy… all conspiring against him for doing one wrong thing.

One thing.

He could still see his father's cold, angry face telling

him to shape up or move out. *"I hired a private investigator. No more, do you hear? No more."*

A private investigator. The thought made him sit up and cast a glance around. Was he being watched right now? Visiting Tyler wasn't a crime, but he'd have to be careful from now on.

Harrison drummed a nervous tattoo on his thigh while he thought.

Drugs. Where could he get them? Not his usual sources; they wouldn't extend any more credit and if his father's PI was following him, it would be sure to make it into some report.

So who, then?

Nobody around Hyams Beach. Nobody in Huskisson; he'd been there too often.

A thought struck him.

Maybe that guy Chad? The one Jason Hoy shared a house with down in Sussex Inlet?

A slow smile grew on his face, and some of the fury mounting inside him eased.

Yeah, Chad whatever his name was, the one who had set himself up as a personal trainer. Harrison had met him only once when he'd bumped into the guy with Jason at the weekend markets. The next time they met up, something Jason had said made it clear that Chad was part of the supply chain. And Harrison had a feeling that was where Tyler had taken his mother's pendant, although he'd been oddly cagey about it.

Harrison sat there for a moment, thinking about the various problems complicating his life and how he could deal with them. If he spun a good enough story, dropped his old man's name, he should be able to cadge enough for tonight. Then, with a few promises, he might be able to set up a future supply too. Kill two birds with one stone.

But first, he'd go home and change into an athletic singlet and shorts and cross-trainers, making it look good. If this private detective was still on the job, it would all look innocent.

Just going to see a trainer, man, to get buff.

He started the engine and backed out of Tyler's driveway.

In Sussex Inlet, Georgie and Scott were drinking coffee in a waterfront tavern with a more inviting menu than the Riverfront Pub'n'Grub.

"So far, you don't have a plan, right?" Scott said.

"I have *kind* of a plan," she corrected him. "Follow Jason, see where he lives, see what his house buddy looks like."

"How, exactly? Throw a rock on the roof and see if he comes out? Peer through a window?"

"All right, it's not much of a plan." Placidly, she took another sip of coffee. "But Jason is… significant. I know it. And I have a feeling that this housemate of his is important. I need to see him."

"Ask him to put on a yellow polo shirt," Scott advised. "And a floppy hat. Then tell him to turn his back, see if he looks like the guy in the crystal ball."

Georgie swatted him on the arm. "Very funny."

"I was thinking," Scott said, "if we find out where he lives *before* Jason goes home, you could knock on the door. Say you're selling life insurance or something." He paused. "Maybe shake hands."

Georgie nodded, seeing where he was coming from. Sometimes, if she made skin-to-skin contact with someone, she'd get a flood of impressions. "Hmm. Yes. See, that's why I'm the psychic, and you're the detective. Your job is to come up with a strategy."

He eyed her narrowly. "This is too easy."

She grinned at him. "All right, I was already thinking along the same lines. I'm not totally ditzy." She took out her phone, brought up contacts, and then tapped on Allie's name, added just the day before. She put it on loudspeaker so Scott could hear too.

Allie answered right away. "Georgie?"

"Hi, Allie. I have a question for you. Our friend Jason Hoy... do you know where he lives?"

"If he's in the same house as when he worked for us, he's over in Summit Avenue. Near the end, a small blue house. I've only been there once, but it was a mess. Junk out the front, overgrown garden."

"Okay. And do you know anything about his housemate?"

"Chad somebody or other," she said. "He works at a couple of gyms around here, but he's set up on his own, so I hear. Used to be Drew's personal trainer."

A light went on in Georgie's mind. "Ah. So that's how Jason knew about an opening for a canoe instructor? Drew said something? And then Chad told Jason?"

"I don't know. Could be. I can ask Drew if you like."

"Maybe later," Georgie said, satisfied. She was always happier when she could see the pieces falling into place. "What do you know about Chad?"

"Nothing, except he's one of those muscle-bound

types, working out all the time. I don't think Drew worked with him for long."

"Thanks." Sensing the other woman's curiosity, she said, "I don't have anything to tell you yet, I'm afraid. Just trying to see where everyone fits in—but I'll keep you posted."

"Sure." Allie sounded a little disappointed. "You, um, haven't done any more crystal ball readings?"

"Not so far. But I'll try again tonight," Georgie promised.

"Thank you. Well…goodbye."

Georgie put her phone away and looked at Scott. "She's hoping I can do something. I always get a bit nervous when I realize how much people count on me sometimes. I mean, nothing's guaranteed."

Scott leaned over and kissed her on the nose. "Nothing's guaranteed with accredited PI's or experienced police detectives, either. But you have an advantage. You can put together the pieces *and* get extra help from woo-woo land."

"Woo-woo land," she said, smiling wryly. "Sounds so professional. I must tell Great Grandma Rosa that eight generations of The Sight have come to this."

"Drink your coffee," he said, "and we'll go looking for a blue house with a messy garden."

Back from his almost-indigestible pub lunch, out in the detached garage he'd outfitted as a gym, with music blaring in his earbuds, Chad Royston didn't realize he had a visitor until someone appeared in the open doorway and waved to get his attention.

That'd be right, he thought in irritation, continuing to pound the treadmill: smack bang in the middle of a new circuit he was trying out. He waved back to let the figure silhouetted against the light know he'd seen him and ran for another two minutes before hitting the pause button on both the treadmill and his music.

The figure stepped forward, and Chad abruptly stopped toweling the sweat from his face as he recognized him.

Harrison Burns. What the hell did *he* want?

"Harrison," he said. "Long time no see. What can I do for you?"

The boy grinned. "So you remember me? You're looking as fit as ever, Chad. Maybe I should sign up. You taking new clients?"

Chad looked him up and down, not attempting to hide his skepticism. Harrison Burns was known for taking the easy way out.

"Anyone I take on has to bust his butt. No pain, no gain. Doubt you'd be up for that."

Harrison kept the smile pasted on his face, but there was a flash of annoyance in his eyes. "You'd be surprised at what I'm up for."

Chad shrugged. "Can we make this quick, Harrison? I'm in the middle of a workout."

"I'll wait." The kid jerked a thumb back over his shoulder in the direction of the house. "I can watch TV or something until you've finished."

Chad almost laughed. Like he was going to let this bozo in the house unsupervised. "Just tell me what you want."

Harrison frowned. Clearly, the conversation wasn't

going the way he wanted. "It'll take more than a few minutes."

"Sorry," Chad said, slinging the towel around his neck and turning away. "I've got to keep going."

"How long will you be?"

Chad gritted his teeth and looked at his watch. "Twenty, twenty-five minutes."

"Okay, then. I'll come back. You will be here, right?"

"Yeah." Without looking at him again, Chad moved to the weight bench and settled himself in position. He waited, hands locked around the bar, until he heard the sound of retreating footsteps.

Harrison bloody Burns. The kid was trouble, and his father was way too connected for Chad's liking. If anything went wrong, the old man would be calling in the cavalry. And if that happened, mud would stick to Chad Royston, not the Burns family.

9

Undercover

WITH THE COUPLE asking questions at the pub, followed by a visit from Harrison, Chad's day was not going well. His mind wasn't on the new routine, so he gave up and went inside for a shower and to think about what Harrison Burns might want.

He had a fair idea.

And what was he going to do about Jason? He weighed up the pros and cons. Jason was useful to him; there was no doubt about that. Not only had he forged several contacts through his work at the pub, but he was prepared to travel to surrounding towns. He was cunning and knew enough to stay under the radar but not so much that he could implicate Chad when it came to bigger deals. However, it was becoming increasingly obvious that he could be the weak link in the chain.

After mulling it over for a while, he decided on an approach. All right: when Harrison came, Chad would make it clear that he was *not* a supplier. No, he would adopt the role of a dedicated personal trainer who was all about pushing your body to peak performance without drugs. He'd take the high road: just because he shared a house with Jason Hoy didn't mean that he approved of drugs. He wasn't Jason's keeper: he couldn't help what he got up to.

It was unlikely that Harrison would swallow that story, thanks to Jason, so maybe he could tell him to try that kid who'd been seen hanging around the Husky pub, dealing. While Chad was prepared to take steps to guard his territory, he was happy enough to let a few minor players have a piece of the action. They made convenient fall guys.

Toweling his hair vigorously, Chad went to the window to watch for Harrison. Part of him thought that he should have told the kid to go away and not return, but if someone was watching the Burns kid, it would be better for him to stay true to the role of a personal trainer. After all, that's what Harrison had been asking about.

Outside, a white four-wheel drive cruised past. Chad squinted at it, trying to see who was driving. Call him suspicious, but it seemed to be going a bit slowly for a casual passer-by.

He stood back from the window and a little to one side, waiting. It had come from the direction of the town, but Harrison still hadn't returned, so the 4WD was unlikely to be following the kid. Of course, it could be just someone on the phone, driving slowly while they were talking.

After a few minutes, the same car went by again, going the other way. This time, he caught a glimpse of the passenger, her face turned towards his house.

He recognized her instantly. It was the American woman from the pub.

Dammit. He hurled the towel aside, fear spiking in his gut. *I knew it.* He hadn't got this far without having a sixth sense about nosy strangers.

They had to be cops.

***

Barely five minutes later, a Prius pulled up out front. Harrison Burns got out and jogged up the path, dodging overgrown bushes on the way. Moments later, Chad heard a confident rap on the door. He answered it and looked at Harrison unsmilingly.

"Hey, man." Harrison reached out a closed fist to bump knuckles. "All finished?"

Chad ignored the fist and pointed to the path that led around the side of the house. "I'll meet you around at the gym, okay?"

Harrison's smile stayed in place, but his eyes grew hard. "That's where you keep the stuff?"

"That's where I keep everything important to me," Chad said. "I just need to get something; only be a moment." With a sharp nod, he closed the door in Harrison's face. Just doing that gave him a jab of satisfaction. He hated entitled little pricks like Harrison Burns.

He found the file he wanted on the computer, hit the print button, and waited while the printer spat out half a dozen pages of generic advice on training. Later, he would enter into his business records that Harrison Burns had come to see him for advice on a get-fit program.

When he reached his backyard gym, Harrison had picked up a 2-kg weight and was doing some arm curls.

He grinned at Chad as he walked in. "Am I doing this right?"

"Too fast," Chad said. "If you're serious about getting fit, you have to do it the right way." He indicated the second chair at a desk he'd wedged into a corner. "Sit down."

Harrison put down the weight and sat down. His eyes were overly bright, and when he sat down, he jiggled a knee up and down. Chad recognized the signs of someone who needed a hit. Ignoring that, he handed Harrison the sheaf of papers. "I've printed out some advice about training in general. Go through it, and see if it sounds like something you are prepared to commit to."

Harrison took the papers with a frown. "Thanks. Maybe one day. What about the other stuff, man?"

"Other stuff?"

"You know what I mean."

Chad leaned back and folded his arms. "Harrison, I don't know what you've heard, but I'm not into drugs. Not steroids, not recreational–nothing. I'm just a personal trainer. If I can't help you with that, then you're in the wrong place."

For a moment, he thought Harrison was going to leap out of the chair and punch him. He tensed and placed his weight on his feet, ready to spring up and defend himself, but Harrison found some measure of control from somewhere, visibly reining himself in. "Come on, mate. You worried I'm going to say some-thing to someone? I know you've got the goods. I need a hit bad, mate."

"I don't deal drugs," Chad said again. "Never have, never will." His eyes went to Harrison's grubby shirt, wondering if there was a wire hidden beneath it. Sure, the guy needed a hit, but that didn't mean the cops hadn't recruited him. "Personal trainers like me, we always have to face suspicion. Too many athletes have used performance-enhancing drugs. They give us all a bad name."

Harrison wasn't having any. "Jason said he got them from you. And I bet Tyler has too, hasn't he?"

"Then I'll be having a word with Jason," Chad said heatedly. "Clearly, he's protecting his real supplier. If he's implicating me, then it might be time I found myself a new housemate." He nodded at the information he printed out. "I can see you're a mess, man. My advice is: get off the drugs, get fit, get a life. But I can't help you."

Parked just down the road in the shade of an old tree, Georgie and Scott heard the angry screech as the Prius backed out of Chad's driveway, with Chad standing at the open door watching him go. A moment later, Harrison roared past them, his jaw set.

"And that," Georgie said, "is why I wanted to come in person. If I hadn't, we wouldn't have seen Chad's visitor. Interesting, is it not?"

Scott drew a checkmark in the air. "Score another one for the good guys. Are you still going to call in and pretend you're selling insurance?"

"No need. Judging by the way Harrison peeled out of there, I'm guessing he didn't get what he wanted. And we now know there's a connection between all three of them." Georgie settled back in her seat. "Let's go."

Scott looked at her quizzically. "Go where?"

"Back to Huskisson," Georgie said with certainty. "And wait. Things are happening."

10

Too Many Questions

WHEN JASON GOT HOME after his shift at the pub, he found a tightly-coiled housemate waiting to pounce.

He'd never seen Chad so annoyed—or so worried. And that was saying something, because they had had a couple of close shaves with stupid kids who were determined to get the drugs they needed no matter what.

"I told you to be careful, didn't I?" Chad was clearly struggling to rein in his emotions.

Jason felt his gut clench. The more controlled Chad was, the more dangerous he was. He had felt the sharp edge of Chad's temper a few times when they were growing up a few doors apart, back in Sydney.

Here in Sussex Inlet, Jason hadn't experienced Chad's anger first hand, unlike some people he'd heard about. He could tell that Chad was getting sick of having him as a housemate. If they hadn't been such good mates as kids, Chad probably would have kicked him out by now.

"I *have* been careful, man," he said defensively, swallowing hard when he thought of the way Chad had slashed a finger across his throat in the pub earlier. "Why, what's happened?"

"I told you that I'd had word from Sydney that there were coppers around, digging into the trade down this way. Undercover. Didn't I?"

"Yeah, you told me. And like I told you, I *have* been careful. I can pick cops. What's going on?" Jason stared at him. Something major was biting Chad. But no matter how he wracked his brains, Jason couldn't think of anything he'd done wrong.

His mind ranged over his customers, mostly people who came to the pub so he could slip them something. There hadn't been anyone new sounding him out for the stuff that Chad handled. They were all regulars, and none of them were likely to talk to the cops.

Nope. His conscience was clear. Frowning, he shook his head at Chad. "If someone's onto you, it ain't through me."

Chad sent him a hard stare. "I was in the pub today, remember?"

"I know, I saw you." Chad liked to sit in a corner, Jason knew, eating his meal and pretending to read the paper while he checked out the scene. On occasions, he would sit there for ages, with an empty plate and a drained glass in front of him, without bothering to acknowledge Jason's presence.

Jason had an uneasy feeling that Chad might some-times be doing it to check up on *him*. Which kind of stuck in his craw because he'd never given him any reason to doubt him.

"And while I was sitting in the pub," Chad said in a dangerously civil tone, "I heard you talking to that

American chick. And the bloke with her. They were asking a lot of questions."

Jason thought back to the conversation with the two people who had come in for a drink. The American girl wasn't exactly someone you'd forget; accents like hers weren't that common in Sussex Inlet. "Not really. What do you mean?"

"I heard them." Chad's patience was running low. "Asking you if you'd worked for Chris Moore and how long you'd been here." Chad's voice grew even quieter, but there was considerable heat there. "You don't think those are odd questions to be asking, in view of what happened?"

Jason stared at him. "You're not trying to tell me that you think *they* were undercover?" He felt queasy, but at the same time, skeptical. He'd never seen those two before, but they were typical of most of the tourists who turned up. They all liked to talk… and what had they said, after all? Only that they'd been out kayaking around the Basin. It was natural that they'd mention who they'd gone with.

He said as much to Chad. "Nah, man. You're barking up the wrong tree. They're nothing but tourists. Just hired Chris Moore to take them around the Basin for the day, that's all."

"And you had to open your big mouth and tell them about drugs in the program! What, are you crazy or something?" Chad's fists clenched. "I have to consider whether I can trust you. I can't afford to keep anyone around who is going to bring us all down."

"You're wrong." Jason made his voice confident, although the churning in his stomach belied his tone. "I tell you, it's nothing."

Chad walked to the window and pointed out at the street. "If it's nothing, maybe you can tell me why they were driving past here earlier? Why they went up the road and then came back again, checking out this place?"

Briefly, Jason closed his eyes. Oh no. *No.* Had he blown it?

"It's got to be a coincidence, that's all," he said nervously. "Just tourists, checking out the town."

"Yeah, sure. Checking out the town, which just happened to take them right past *this* place." Chad turned around, fixing Jason with a heated glare. "And the very same day, Harrison Burns turns up here looking for a supply of whatever makes him happy. Too many coincidences for my liking." His voice grew more menacing. "I've worked hard to set things up here, building up my business into something legit to have a profile in the community. I don't want it all to be ruined because of you."

Defeated, Jason shook his head. "Sorry, man. I didn't know. You know I wouldn't dump you in it. We go way back, don't we?"

"Which is why you're still here. But don't count on past friendship to get you out of this."

Chad paced the room and held up his hand when Jason went to say something else. "Be quiet. I'm thinking."

Finally, he stopped and looked at Jason speculatively. "You still in contact with Drew Moore?"

"Not for a while. He pretty much cut me dead after the Harrison Burns business." Resentment edged Jason's voice.

"Well, you'll have to think of a reason to go see him

again. We need to find out more about the two that came into the pub today. If they were out with his dad, then he'll be able to tell you something about them. Once we know who they are and what they're doing here, then I can figure out what to do next."

He moved across to stand in front of Jason, his eyes colder than Jason had ever seen them. "See Drew, find out who they were, then come back and tell me."

"Sure." Jason had no idea how he would make that happen, but he wasn't about to argue with Chad in his present mood.

"Do it now."

"Fine. Fine." Jason threw his hands up in the air. "I'll go now."

He spun on his heel and slammed out of the back door, down the steps, and along the path, striding back to his car.

If Chad was right, and those two in the pub had been undercover, then he'd screwed up. Well, he didn't need to be caught up in any police investigation of what was going on down here in Sussex Inlet. He'd try to find out who those two were, and if it looked like things were getting too hot, he was out of here.

He owed Chad Royston nothing.

Jason found Drew's wife Emma sitting at the counter of their boat repair business, filling in some ledger. She glanced up at him, and her normally cheerful face developed a pinched look right away. That got Jason's back up for a start. Snippy little thing, Emma Moore; thought she was too good for the likes of him.

"Hi Emma," he said cordially. "Drew around, by any chance?"

"No," she said coolly. "He's out quoting on a job."

"When do you expect him back?"

"No idea. After that, he was off to Nowra to do some work on a boat." Her eyes returned to the ledger, and she continued making notes.

"Oh, okay. Well, I might pop in tomorrow. Can you tell him I called?"

Emma flicked him a glance, gave the barest hint of a nod, and then kept writing. Jason gave her a dirty look, which was a wasted effort because she didn't see it. He'd gritted his teeth, bid her a friendly farewell, and left—no point in antagonizing her before he had a chance to talk to Drew.

He'd call back tomorrow, and Chad would just have to wait for the information he wanted.

Jeez, was he ever *over* this town.

11

An Invitation

THE NEXT MORNING, Drew Moore looked up when the bell above the door dinged, and smiled at the two who entered.

His mother, dressed in her usual soft, comfortable clothes, swished in ahead of his father. Her face was bright, and she had a grin from ear to ear. Chris's gaze moved to his dad, coming in behind her. As usual, he didn't look happy with life. Sure, he tried to hide it and put a good face on things, but Chris could see the change in him. His father was growing old before his eyes.

Drew's stomach twisted with anxiety. Everyone's lives had changed so much over a short six months.

He didn't know if things could ever be the same again. But if *he* had anything to do with it, things would turn around. They had to.

He forced a grin and leaned forward so his mother could give him the usual kiss on the cheek.

"Drew!" Her face was alive. "We've just come from a meeting about the inaugural Seasonal Markets. It's going to be such a great thing for the town! There are all sorts of things happening, and if they do well, we'll get people coming from miles around every time we have them! We're thinking markets once a month, in a range of locations, but then really big ones with every change of season."

"That's great, Mum. You've been trying to make this happen for years." He looked at his father and was pleased to see him shaking his head at Allie, a wry grin on his face.

"You know what your mother's like once she gets the bit between her teeth," his father said. "I don't know why they just don't make her the mayor and be done with it."

"Oh, you." Allie dug him in the ribs. "Well, you know how I am about my crafts and the markets. It's my passion."

Chris and his father exchanged a grin. In unison, they said: "We know." In their family, it had always been a bit of an inside joke about the bits of twine and string and filmy scarves and bits and pieces of jewelry his mother liked to make in her spare time. Even in the busy early days when she and Chris had been building up the business and looking after small children, there had always been time for craft.

"Anyway." His mother dug into her embroidered shoulder bag. "I've got something for you. You were asking about photos? Dad taking groups out on the Basin, kayaking? I've got *tons* of great photos here. What are you going to do with them?"

Drew accepted the bright green USB stick she handed over. He had no idea whether the social media posts he was planning would have any effect. They couldn't do any harm. Okay, so his father didn't know how to use any of this stuff, but it was easy enough to learn.

"I'm going to put some on the Facebook page I set up," he said. "And I'm posting to Instagram, too. I started doing that a while back, for this business, and you'd be surprised how many people pass around the information they see on these accounts. I've put up photos of boats I've restored, comments from happy customers, some just showing boats out with people having fun fishing, boating on the Basin. That kind of thing. And I'm going to use them in memes too." He caught himself and laughed, seeing the confusion on both parents' faces. "Don't worry about it. A meme, it's… you know those quotes you see with pictures of cute kittens doing funny things? And inspirational quotes from business leaders? There's usually a picture and some quote or funny comment. People forward them to other people on social media. On Facebook."

His mother's eyes brightened with comprehension. "Oh, like those things that Aunt Casey is always sending me!"

"Exactly," Drew said.

"Great," his mother said, nodding. "Sounds like a wonderful idea, Drew. Those things get sent on to heaps of people."

"That's why it's called viral media. They keep getting passed on, like a virus."

He wasn't surprised to see his father's eyes glazing over. Chris Moore wasn't exactly a computer illiterate, but he just didn't care.

Oh well. It didn't matter whether he understood

what happened behind the scenes; it only mattered that it could help revive the business.

Drew slid the USB stick into his pocket. "I'll do something with this tonight, guys. Then I'll send it to you, so you can see what I mean."

"That would be fantastic. And, Drew? You and Emma are coming to dinner tonight." His mother looked mischievous. "We've got a special treat in store."

Happy to see his mother cheerful and more like her old self, he grinned at her. "A surprise? And what might that be? Do I get to know ahead of time?"

"Sure. I've already told Emma, anyway. You'll never guess, Drew." Allie paused for effect, obviously relishing the surprise. "We've got this fantastic person I met from America coming to dinner. She's *amazing*. Do you know she's an eighth-generation gypsy?"

Drew couldn't help it; he had to laugh. This was so much like his mother. She had always been a bit of a flake, but this? An eighth-generation gypsy was coming to dinner. It was so up her alley. "Well, that sounds like an interesting dinner guest, all right."

"She's over here with her Australian boyfriend. They're traveling around the country, seeing the sights. But Drew, that's not the most exciting part. She's brought her crystal ball with her, and she's already done a reading for us." His mother cast a brief, wary look at her husband. "You won't *believe* what she sees in that crystal ball."

Drew saw that his father's face had closed up, and he had that tight, worried look again. A tremor of anxiety ran through him. He didn't believe in this stuff, but… what had she seen?

"I know you guys don't believe in this, but Drew,

she's the real thing." Allie hesitated but went on anyway. "She saw actual *people* in the crystal ball, and we could see them too! And the things that she knew…." Finally, she stopped. "But you'll see for yourself. Emma's going to love her!"

Feeling as though events were spiraling out of control, Drew just nodded. "Okay. Uh, sounds great, Mum."

"Come over as soon as you've closed up the business, we'll have a quick meal, and a chat before Georgie and Scott get there. This is going to be fun."

The door chime sounded, and a customer walked in. Drew had never been so glad to see a client in his life.

"Alright," he said. "We'll see you tonight, then."

His mother stepped aside to let the customer come up to the counter and waved at him. "See you later."

Drew summoned up a smile for the customer but spared one last glance at his mother whisking out of the door, with his dad trailing after her.

An eighth-generation gypsy with a crystal ball?

Images of Chad Royston flashed into his mind.

He didn't want anyone to know that he and Chad once used to do business—business other than getting fit, that is. His father had always been so outspoken about drugs and athletes who used steroids. Drew had cut all ties with Chad Royston after that disastrous school expedition; he had stopped training and bulking up completely. His CrossFit mates had asked why he'd stopped, but Drew had just shrugged and said he didn't have time to run a business and work out.

He had a feeling they knew there was more to it. His father's name had been part of the neighborhood gossip for months. But they'd accepted it, and now he rarely saw them.

Mechanically, Drew looked after his customer's needs, but his mind was elsewhere.

A gypsy who saw things in a crystal ball. As if things weren't bad enough.

An hour later, Jason walked through the door. Today, he had made sure that Drew's ute was in the parking lot before he came in. The office was empty, but out the back, he could hear someone moving around.

"Drew? Hey man, you got a minute?" Jason moved past the reception area to the work bay, to find Drew straightening up from something he was doing to an outboard motor. When he looked at Jason, his face didn't look any friendlier than his wife's had the day before.

"I'm pretty busy, actually," he said. He stood facing Jason with his arms loose at his sides, an oily rag dangling from his fingers. Then he wiped his hands and tossed the rag behind him. "What is it, Jason?"

His attitude irked Jason. Okay, so Drew's old man's business had suffered a hit after the drugs thing, but was it *Jason's* fault that idiots like Harrison Burns couldn't be controlled?

Still, he kept a grin on his face and shoved his hands in his pockets to give off a casual air. "Well, this won't take long. I have a few people at the pub from time to time asking about who they can get to fix their boats, you know? And I've been meaning to say to you, leave your business cards with me, and maybe I can send some business your way."

"Thanks, but I think Emma has already been around to the pubs and café's, leaving business cards. And she has put up flyers at the IGA supermarket."

"Well, it won't hurt to give me a few more," Jason offered, trying a friendly smile again. "I can keep them with me, give them to people."

Jason watched Drew's brows draw together in a frown and knew he'd gone too far. Drew knew that Jason didn't care enough about him to come in and volunteer to hand out business cards.

Before Drew could send him away, Jason gestured around him at the tidy workshop. "Business going well, is it?"

"Well enough."

Drew wasn't doing anything to help him out here. Tamping down his annoyance, Jason decided to cut to the chase. "Had an interesting couple coming to the pub for lunch yesterday. An American woman and her Aussie boyfriend."

"Did you?"

"Yeah. She said she had been kayaking around the Basin with your dad. He took them on one of those day tours. They said they had a great time." He tried another smile. "That's what made me think of you, though that maybe I could help out by putting some business your way. Like, no hard feelings, okay?"

"No hard feelings?" Drew let out a humorless crack of laughter. "You ruin my dad's life, and now you're saying no hard feelings? You've got to be kidding."

Tossing pretense aside, Jason glared back at him. "You're no clean-skin, though, are you, Drew Moore?

You used to be happy enough to get your supplies from Chad."

"And I never went near him again, after that. But a few steroids are nothing like what you did."

This was getting nowhere. Laying his cards on the table, Jason said, "Chad is worried about that American. He thinks she might not be who she says she is. Not really a tourist." Jason took a step closer to Drew. "If undercover cops are down here poking around, it will come back on you too. On *anyone* who has had dealings with Chad."

Drew stared at him and then laughed again. "Undercover cops? You're an idiot, Jason. Do you know who that woman is? She's a *gypsy*. She travels around with a crystal ball, telling fortunes. Mum's already had a reading, and now she's lined up another one for tonight. Does that sound like an undercover cop to you?" He shook his head. "Just get out, Jason. And don't come in here again. I'd rather go broke than have any business come my way through you." He turned his back on him and started poking around under the engine cowling again.

Jason imagined picking up the engine and slamming Drew over the head with it but instead turned and strode out. Despite Jason's open hostility, he'd got what he had come for.

Undercover cop? He grinned to himself as he thought of what he'd report back to Chad.

Try fortune-telling gypsy, Chad. Relief swept through him. It looked like they had dodged a bullet this time, and he wouldn't have to leave town in a hurry.

12

The Players Gather

WHEN GEORGIE AND SCOTT ARRIVED, they followed the sound of voices and found Allie and Chris sitting out back with their son and his wife, drinks in hand, sharing a laugh about something. Allie jumped up and gave them both a quick hug before turning to her son and his wife. "Georgie, I'd like to introduce you to our son Drew and his wife, Emma." She squeezed Georgie's arm. "I've been telling them what a treat they have in store."

One look at Drew's face gave her a fair idea of his attitude towards fortune-tellers: before he hid his feelings with a polite smile, he wore the same expression that she'd seen on Chris's face the first night—the *"I don't want to be here, but I'll go along with it"* look.

Well, she couldn't say she wasn't used to that. In all the time she'd been reading people's futures in the crystal ball—and seeing far too many secrets revealed about people who had something to hide—she had been observing that same caution on some faces.

But, she thought, looking at him again, Drew wasn't

just skeptical. There was a hint of apprehension in his eyes.

Interesting.

"Hi." Georgie smiled at Drew and Emma and then reached for Scott. "I've been looking forward to meeting you both! This is Scott."

"Hi." Scott smiled his easy grin and shook hands with both of them. "Lovely spot you've chosen to live in here."

"Yes, we both like the Basin," Drew said, forcing a smile.

Georgie didn't miss Emma's glance at him as he spoke. Although he'd said he liked living there, she could sense the tension underlying his words. Was Drew in some trouble?

She gave no outward sign of the thoughts buzzing through her mind. Letting her thoughts drift, she sensed… changes. Maybe Drew and Emma were planning to move away but didn't want his parents to know yet, given all the heartache they'd had.

Don't start analyzing people yet, Georgie, she told herself. *What is meant to be, is meant to be.*

"I've so been looking forward to this," Emma told her, clearly bubbling with excitement. "Allie says you're the real thing." Instantly, her hand went to her mouth. "Oh, I didn't mean——"

"That I might be a fake?" Georgie grinned back at her, liking her instantly. Emma had one of those vibrant faces people just take to: curly red hair gathered up with the giant clip, so that little tendrils fell around her face; a wide grin and dancing eyes. "Don't feel bad. I know what you mean. Unfortunately, there are people around who take advantage of others. Don't worry. This will be just for fun." Her words were as much to put Drew at ease as to reassure Emma, but she took care not to look at him.

"You really have your great-grandma's crystal ball? And she used to travel in a real gypsy trailer?"

"I do, and she did."

"Sit down, relax and have a drink first," Allie suggested, waving them at a couple of comfortable camp chairs. "Wine, beer, or soft drinks?"

"Wine for me." Georgie settled herself in the chair and watched Allie and Emma fetch more drinks. Clearly, the two of them got on famously. They were even dressed alike: long soft cotton skirts, tank tops, and light-weight cardigans against the evening chill.

Scott accepted a beer and looked at Drew. "Chris tells me you have a boat repair business? That sounds like a good choice in a place like St Georges Basin."

Responding to his friendly grin, Drew nodded and started telling him about how it all started. Within a few minutes, he was looking much more relaxed.

Allie's suggestion to have a few drinks and a chat before the reading was a good idea, Georgie thought. Almost an hour later, when the six of them settled around the table, everyone seemed relaxed.

Until she uncovered the crystal ball.

Georgie smiled around at them, reading their faces. Allie was as keen as mustard, although Georgie could sense the underlying anxiety. Allie, wanting their lives to be back to what they were, was desperate to find out what lay in her future. Georgie felt a pang at the thought. Sometimes, the responsibility of what she did weighed heavily.

Her gaze moved to Chris, sitting next to Allie. He

caught her eye and gave a small smile. Clearly, he didn't expect anything to come out of tonight, but he was resigned to whatever the evening should reveal. And then, right next to him, his son Drew.

Drew, staring at the crystal globe, was radiating nervousness. Georgie's smile didn't waver, but she found herself wondering again what it was that had him so uptight. Most often, when people didn't like the idea of a reading, it was because they had something to hide.

Earlier, as they'd all chatted while watching the moon rise and reflect off the water, Georgie had covertly observed him. Talking about his plans for his father's Facebook page and Instagram, he seemed like a pleasant man who cared about his parents and his wife. But there was no mistaking his skittishness. There was *something* there.

And then there was Emma. She was looking at Georgie expectantly, a grin stretching wide across her face. The faint smattering of freckles on her nose seemed to dance in anticipation, and her eyes gleamed.

As their eyes met, Georgie felt a sudden connection to the girl on the other side of the table. Then, coming to her with complete certainty, Georgie thought: *she's pregnant.* The thought gave her pleasure: Emma would make a great mother.

Georgie glanced down at the crystal ball, her hands automatically moving to cup the shining globe. Did Emma *know* that she was pregnant? She would have to be careful here: no breaking news before people were ready. Maybe she could hint that there was a child in the future and see what Emma said.

The moment her hands touched the crystal ball, her certainty about Emma's condition grew even stronger.

But this time, feelings flowed into her as well: joy, anticipation, and then, amazingly, the image of a bouncy little redheaded toddler, a girl with tanned skin and a riot of deep auburn curls, with blue eyes just like her mother's. Georgie risked another glance at Emma, unable to stop a smile. This child was going to bring an enormous amount of joy to the family.

It was nice to start with such a positive image. And it augured well for the rest of the evening. She had times when she fought to get anything at all. Sometimes, like tonight, images and impressions came in a steady flow. She moved her hands and stared down into the depths of the crystal ball. There was nothing there yet but the usual white mist starting to swirl and form inside. There was no image of a child; her knowledge of the babe growing in Emma's womb came from that certainty within her.

She felt Scott's elbow nudge her from the side and looked up to find four sets of eyes focused on her.

"I've already told Allie and Chris how this goes," she said. "Sometimes I see images; sometimes not. At times, *you* may see pictures in the crystal ball too, but not everyone does. Often, I just hear or see words form in my mind. Sometimes it's auditory; sometimes I *see* words." She looked at Emma and Drew. "I know all of this must sound odd if you haven't experienced it before." Georgie made a funny face and cast a wry look around at them all. "I wish I could explain it, understand it more, myself. Half the time, *I'm* trying to work out how this stuff comes to me."

She took a deep breath. "Okay. I can just tell you what I pick up, and then maybe one of you can share if it seems to have any bearing on your life—or if you like, you can ask *me* questions. We can go around the group one by one, or…." She shrugged. "It can be pretty much whatever you want it to be."

Unexpectedly, Drew broke in. "And what if you see anything—uh, bad? Something that you don't want to tell us? Do you tell us anyway, or do you hold stuff back?"

That was an odd thing to ask at the beginning of a reading. The impression that Drew was hiding something, or protecting someone, grew. Keeping her face impassive, she just nodded at him. "Good question. I have to admit; I haven't often seen anything too bad. If you're wondering if I can foretell something like the day you're going to die, or if something terrible is going to befall you, it's not likely." She smiled. "Sometimes, I can warn people if I see something bad coming down the track. On rare occasions, I've been able to see what it is, but for me, it's more like a puzzle that I've got to put together. I see the shapes; I get impressions, I put them together."

"Like a detective," Allie said with a grin.

"It sometimes works like that," Georgie said. "But sometimes, it's not me; it's *you* that has to be the detective. What I see might not have any meaning for me." Out of the corner of her eye, she saw Drew stiffen.

Beside her, Scott broke in. "Probably better if we just get started, hey, Georgie?"

Good old Scott. He always knew when to step in and make things easier. She glanced around. "Okay. Does anyone want to start, or will I just see what comes up first?"

Emma put her hand in the air and then pulled it

down hastily when everyone broke into laughter. "Can I go first?"

Georgie grinned at her, knowing what she was probably going to ask. "Sure. What would you like to know?"

"Um…" Emma threw a sideways look at Drew and then across at Allie. "I was just wondering… Drew and I, we're kind of thinking of having three, maybe four children." She shrugged. "Yeah, I know, everyone tells me that as soon as I have the first one, I might change my mind about three or four. But to be kinda fun to know." She wrinkled her nose at Drew, who was rolling his eyes. "Um, can you tell us anything about that?"

Amidst general laughter, Georgie nodded. She glanced back at the crystal ball, but there was still no image there: just the familiar white mist, swirling slowly around the middle. That in itself was enough to have Allie's and Chris's eyes riveted on the crystal ball. They knew this happened before images started to form.

Allie sat forward with a wriggle of excitement. "I'd like to know that too. Imagine me a Grandma!" She peered into the depths of the crystal ball, squinting her eyes. "Do you think we would be able to see them in the crystal ball? Like we saw Harrison and Jason?"

Allie didn't miss Drew shifting in his chair when he heard that, but she also heard Scott's quiet chuckle beside her at Allie's words, which made her grin too. "You might, but don't get your hopes up. There's nothing there yet."

She looked up, and her eyes met Emma's, and instantly the number 3 formed in her mind. Again, she had a mental image of the laughing little redheaded girl. And then two more babies appeared: these were girls too, but they looked more like Drew, with steady eyes and nut-brown hair. Two little girls, like peas in a pod. Georgie smiled.

"You know," Emma said, staring at her. "You do, don't you? You *know.*"

Know what? Georgie thought. *Know that you're pregnant already, or know that you'll have three little girls?*

Both, she thought, but she didn't say that. "Emma… You do know that I can't guarantee any of this, don't you?" Georgie moved one hand off the crystal ball and reached across to lay her hand gently on Emma's. The moment she did, she could feel that she was right. "But yes, I see three children in your future."

Emma beamed at her. "Can you tell me anything about them? You know, if they're boys or girls? And… and do you know *when?*"

Georgie thought of the images she had seen: the bubbly little toddler with red hair and the two smaller babies.

"I feel you're going to have a girl first," she said. "She is going to look a lot like her mother. Red curly hair, but a bit darker than yours, Emma." A gurgle of laughter escaped her. "And she's going to have more energy than a barrel full of monkeys. That one is going to keep you running around; I can promise you that."

"Can you tell how soon?" Emma's hand crept to Drew's and her fingers closed around his. Drew was staring at Georgie with fascination.

"Soon," Georgie said. "Very soon." Her eyes locked with Emma's, and the two of them grinned at each other.

Allie gasped as realization dawned on her face. "Emma! Drew! Have you been holding back on us?"

"No," Drew and Emma said at the same time. They

smiled at each other, and Georgie warmed to see how much love there was there.

"I wasn't sure," Emma said. "I was going to go to the chemist tomorrow and pick up a test." She looked back to Georgie. "But… do you think…?"

Taking that as permission to say what she thought, Georgie nodded. "Yes, I do think so. Congratulations, you two."

At that, everything stopped for the next few minutes while Allie rushed around the table to hug both of them and started suggesting glasses of bubbles after the reading finished—and then amended it hastily to '…but just soft drink for Emma, of course!" while everyone laughed again.

When the hubbub had died down, Georgie found Chris looking at her with a little more respect and openness, but Drew had gone from the happy-new-dad flush of happiness back to being wary.

He now had a taste of what she could do. And he was worried.

"Before we go on," Emma said, "You said… *three*? You saw three?"

Georgie glanced back at the crystal ball. It was still revealing nothing: all the information about Emma and Drew's babies had filtered through what she thought of as a kind of mysterious channel to the universe. Sometimes she pictured all the knowledge in the world, past, and future, out there like a big deep well, waiting to flow through to her if she opened up the channels.

"I didn't see anything in the crystal ball if that's what you mean." She smoothed her hands over the glass surface again, feeling the odd warmth that always came up when she did a reading, and things were flowing.

"Lots of things come *through* the crystal ball: I use it as a way of tapping into possibilities, I guess. But with the baby, I just saw an image in my mind." She smiled at her again. "That can happen when a client is excited about something because the emotions are so strong. It doesn't always happen. I'd say it more often *doesn't*."

"But you said, three children?" Emma persisted. "Can you tell me any more?"

Finally, Drew spoke up. "Do we want to know everything, Emma? Maybe some surprises would be nice?"

Emma looked at Drew and then looked at Georgie. The other woman was jumping with the urge to know. "Drew... I would kind of like to know, I think. And then if it turns out differently, well, we'll get a surprise anyway, won't we?"

Georgie looked at Drew, her brows raised. He waved his hands haplessly, looked at the ceiling, and then nodded. "Fine, go ahead. Tell us whatever you know."

"No promises," Georgie reminded them.

"Fine, fine." Emma waved that away. "Just tell me before I burst."

"Two more girls after the first one," Georgie told her. "And... they were like two peas in a pod. Either you're going to have two little girls very close together, or you're going to have twins."

Emma squealed with delight, and Allie had to jump up out of her seat and go round and give her another hug.

Chris and Drew just looked at each other and shook their heads.

Things settled down again, and Georgie looked around. "Well, does anyone want to go next, or will I just see what comes up?"

Beside her, Georgie sensed Allie becoming tense. She turned her head and looked at her, and Allie gave a quick nod. Georgie read the nod for what it was: Allie wanted to know more about what lay in the future. More about what had happened to rip their lives apart.

She hoped she could help them, but at least she knew they would have a wonderful little granddaughter to fill their lives.

"Just see what comes up, then?" she said. "Okay. If anyone does have any questions, just hold them in your mind. That could influence what I see."

She turned back to the crystal ball.

13

The Mist in the Crystal

GEORGIE CLOSED her eyes for a moment and let her whole body relax. She could tell when she'd entered the zone, as she sometimes thought of it, because she could sense her mind floating away. She wasn't quite sitting there looking down on herself; it wasn't an out-of-body experience, but…it felt different. It was as though the world receded for a moment, and she became aware not so much of the people around her, but a kind of energy field around them.

Even that didn't really sum it up, but the important thing was that mostly, it worked.

It was working now. Georgie curved her fingers around the smooth surface of the crystal ball and let the warmth from it flood into her hands.

It was strange how her abilities kept developing. Once, she had had to exert a lot more effort before messages or impressions would come through. Now, mostly, she just allowed herself to float. She could almost *feel* the questions hovering around her.

She was aware that Allie, beside her, was focusing

hard on understanding what had happened to them and what would come out of it. She could feel Chris, wary but still needing to know. Then there was Emma, radiant with pregnancy and simply…happy. She had found out what she wanted to know; now, she was merely keen to hear anything more about her yet-to-be-born daughters.

She could sense Scott beside her, a rock-like presence as always. His warmth and good humor, and steady support were always there.

And then there was Drew. His anxiety loomed over the other emotions she could feel in this room tonight.

Under her fingers, the crystal ball grew warmer still. Slowly, Georgie opened her eyes and drew her fingers away, knowing there would be something to see.

The white mist had given way to dark, boiling clouds, and in those clouds, she could see vague figures moving. Her brow creasing, she stared harder at the crystal ball, trying to let her eyes see beyond what was visible to everyone else in the room—for a glance around showed that they could all see it: every one of them. Quite often, only one or two of the group were able to see what she saw, but not tonight. Every eye was fixed on the crystal ball in front of her, and she was sorry to see that Emma's joy about her little redheaded daughter was dimming. She wasn't scared, but she was puzzled and a little apprehensive.

Allie's hand closed over her forearm. "Georgie?" Her voice trembled a little. "Georgie? Those dark clouds, what do they mean?"

Georgie stole a glance sideways, coming out of the deep place she had entered to reassure her. "It's all right,

Allie. This doesn't necessarily mean anything. There's nothing to see yet."

And it was true, of a sort. The messages she received didn't have to be what they looked like on the surface. She had discovered that often enough.

She opened her mind again and, almost like flicking a switch, the clouds went from black to grey, the dark figures disappeared, and the crystal ball was full of white mist again. But inside the fog, she could see something.

Letters were forming.

Georgie tilted her head to one side while she regarded them. J and B. But each letter appeared twice. "JB, JB," she said, but nothing came to her. "Could JB stand for Jervis Bay?"

At her words, there was a slight gasp from Chris across the table. Allie glanced up. At the last reading, Chris had said nothing. Now, he drew his brows together in a slight frown. "JB twice?" he said. "I wonder…"

Allie gave a snort of laughter that held no humor. "JB-JB. Well, we know who that is, don't we?"

A glance around the table showed that everyone was nodding. Georgie looked at Chris. "What do you mean? Double JB? Or JB twice? That means something to you?"

"It means something to all of us," Drew said, his mouth snapping closed on the last word before he took a breath and went on. "JB-JB. It stands for Jesse Burns of Jervis Bay. The big man himself. He uses it as a kind of logo. It's even on some of his business cards, JB twice."

Georgie looked at them all interrogatively. "Jesse Burns. I've heard that name."

"Oh yeah, you've heard it all right," said Chris.

"Jesse Burns. The father of that little rat Harrison Burns. Like father, like son."

Georgie nodded slowly, looking at the intertwined letters which were still shining clearly within the depths of the crystal. "I don't know the *exact* questions all of you have in your minds, but it seems clear that this Jesse Burns has got something to do with what you want to know." She looked around. "Anyone?"

"It's answered *my* question," Chris said bitterly. "Which was: 'Who is responsible for everything I've ever worked for falling apart?'" He pointed at the crystal ball. "And to me, that's a clear enough answer. Jesse Burns. Who else would want revenge for the shame brought upon his family by his son? I never liked the man."

Allie sat forward and reached across the table to grab Chris's hand. "Chris, this isn't proof. Please, don't do anything."

He looked at her bleakly. "What exactly do you think I *could* do, Allie? Jesse Burns holds all the power around here. He's on the school board; he's got a wide and influential old-boy network from his private school in Sydney—he's on I don't know how many boards down there as well, for heaven's sake."

There was silence in the room for a moment, then Chris's face changed, as though he'd just heard the significance of his own words echoing in the room. "That's *it*. First, one of my staff members brings in drugs and gives them to that boy. That's the start of it all." The bitterness in his voice was palpable. "Then the school throws Harrison out, and it's the hot topic around here. He blackens the family name, and Jesse Burns blames me. So he finishes me off for no good reason other than he needs revenge." He sat back in his chair and closed his eyes. "*That's* why I haven't had the schools confirming contracts in the New Year. It's Jesse Burns and his old boy network. I should have known it was more than just the schools themselves."

"Dad." Drew put an arm around his father, looking visibly upset. "He might have the power, but you're the one with the good name around here. Ask anyone, and you'll hear the same: you're the one they hold in high esteem, not Jesse Burns. Nobody around here cares about his money."

Chris slumped, looking defeated. "They might not care about money," he said, "and they might not care about Jesse Burns. But can't you see that it doesn't matter? He just doesn't matter anymore. My reputation is ruined, and there is nothing I can do. Nothing." He turned and looked Drew full in the face. "And don't think I don't appreciate all you're trying to do for me, mate. I do. But it's gone. It's all too late." He shook his head again and pushed back his chair. "Sorry. I've got to —" he got up and walked swiftly out of the room.

Georgie looked back at the crystal ball. The logo had disappeared, and instead, she could see a new image. She stared at it and then wrinkled her forehead. "I know that face."

"Me too." Scott's voice came from beside her. "But where from?"

"Yesterday," Georgie said. "That blue house. He was at the door."

Drew leaned forward and stared until he could see what Georgie was looking at. His gaze flew up to meet hers. "It's Chad Royston."

Georgie nodded. "Royston, that's his surname? Scott and I checked out his place yesterday, and guess who we saw stopping in to see him?" She turned to look at Allie and then across to Drew. "Could Chad Royston and Jason be in it together?"

"I wouldn't put it past Jason Hoy," Chris said, still looking shell-shocked. "As I told you, I had to let him go. As for Chad, I don't know." He looked at Drew. "You worked out with him for a while. What do you think?"

Drew shrugged and looked away. "It's possible. I know Chad and Jason were friends as kids."

Looking at the downcast faces of the family who had had their lives ruined, Georgie sighed. "I don't know how helpful any of this is."

Allie's voice came hesitantly, quietly. "But what about those black clouds, Georgie? Do they mean anything now that you've seen the rest?"

The answer came to Georgie instantly, but she didn't want to say it. She glanced across at Drew to find that he was staring at her, with the same question in his eyes. She remembered what he had said earlier: *If you knew something bad, would you tell us?"*

She owed it to him to say something. "Yes," she said reluctantly. She looked at Allie and then at Drew. "I feel… I strongly feel that this isn't over yet. You must all be careful. I think both Harrison Burns and his father can be quite dangerous. Please… don't do anything rash."

14

Allie's Idea

ALLIE FOUND that was no consoling Chris that night.

They tried: after Georgie and Scott left, she opened a bottle of champagne leftover from Christmas, and they toasted the new baby—all except Emma because she was now swearing off alcohol for a while. Although she hadn't had the test yet, everyone was certain that Georgie was right. Allie felt a huge, warm glow of satisfaction roll through her at the thought of a tiny little girl with tumbling red curls, and what Georgie had said when she was staring into the crystal ball, her soft brown eyes warm and her lips curving with laughter: *"…more energy than a barrel full of monkeys."*

It sounded like just what the family needed. New life and a new focus.

In the end, Chris had gone to bed early, and Drew and Emma had headed off home. Allie could tell, looking at Drew, that he blamed himself for introducing Jason Hoy to the family, and all the trouble that followed. Her heart went out to her boy. He was a good son and didn't deserve to have the actions of people like Jason Hoy and Harrison Burns reflecting on him. He'd only been trying to do Jason a favor, pointing him in the direction of some employment. He wasn't to know that Jason would bring drugs into the school program. She had pulled him aside and told him as much, but he had just shaken his head and looked away, but not before she had seen the bleakness in his eyes. He was doing his best to help his father, to resurrect the business, but none of it was going to do any good.

Chris was lost. This latest news about the possible involvement of Jesse Burns seemed to be the nail in his coffin.

A shudder went through her at the phrase. *A nail in his coffin.* It was almost as though the death of his business had been the death of everything Chris lived for as well.

No, there was more to life than that! *New baby*, she reminded herself.

She busied herself for a while, going through the arrangements for the first seasonal markets. This would be a big thing for the Basin: traders coming together from small towns and hamlets all around St Georges Basin. And Sussex Inlet needed it: a sprawling, vibrant riverside market that would bring people from miles around. Chris could advertise there, too…

She sighed. It was going to be difficult to get Chris to agree to anything.

Jesse Burns. Her heart burned with anger at the thought of the man: one of those privileged people who didn't care about trampling on others if necessary to get what he wanted or to preserve his reputation. The moment Chris had looked at Georgie and said: "Jesse

Burns is behind all this," she had known, somewhere deep within, that he was right.

She flipped over some of the papers in her folder about the markets and stared at the hated logo. Jesse Burns was one of the major sponsors for the whole thing. He was providing prizes and signage. He'd even agreed to participate in an ad for the local TV station, talk to some of the farmers market's local producers, and visit local artisans to promote their work.

How were they going to undo the damage that Jesse Burns had done? He was untouchable. If only they had some way of exerting pressure on him, some way of making him acknowledge the harm he had done to one local business.

If it IS him, a small voice inside her warned.

Allie stared into space. She was a live-and-let-live kind of person. She didn't believe in revenge, or trampling the little people, or lining your pockets at the expense of someone else—but that was exactly the kind of thing Jesse Burns did. Now, thanks to Georgie, she was pretty certain that he was behind *their* troubles, too.

All at once, the germ of an idea formed in her mind.

Jesse Burns. Markets. Georgie.

Allie flipped through the folder of applicants and stall owners for the markets. Plenty of craft stalls; jewelry, soaps, wooden signs, wooden toys. Plenty of food tents, too. They were looking at making that a feature: international food. The usual jumping castle for the kids, pony rides, and a lot of local produce for the farmers' market.

Allie felt a jump of excitement. What they *didn't* have was a tarot reader or fortune teller. The usual tarot reader was overseas, visiting her family.

The idea grew and took form in her mind. *Yes. It could be a way...*

She reached for her phone and called Georgie.

Georgie answered right away. "Allie?" There was a thread of anxiety in her voice. "Is Chris all right?" Clearly, she was worried at what the night had revealed.

Not that she could have prevented them all from seeing what was in the crystal ball anyway. That logo: two JBs intertwined...

"He's fine, Georgie," Allie said briskly. "Well, he's depressed, but he's been like that for months now. But Georgie, I have an idea. I was thinking... if you were to talk to Jesse Burns, organize a reading for him, do you think you might be able to find out something we could use?"

There was a silence for a moment, and when she spoke again, Georgie's voice was wary. "Allie, you know I can't guarantee anything. There have been cases where I haven't been able to pick up anything at all. But...even if it were possible to get him to agree to a reading, I'm not quite sure what you intend to do with anything I might find out."

Allie immediately understood what she meant. "Oh, Georgie. Don't worry; I'm not thinking of blackmail or anything like that. Bring myself down to his level? *Never.* But I thought maybe... I don't know what I thought. That there might be something we could investigate further. Something that we can use for leverage." Then she shook her head and sighed. "I guess it sounds a bit like blackmail. I just want something I can use to show him that he can't ride roughshod over everyone all the time. That some of us will fight back."

"I understand." There was another silence, and then

Georgie said, "Allie, even if it is possible to meet with Jesse Burns, I'd have to have the option of keeping anything I find out to myself. It's…an ethical thing."

Much as she liked Georgie, Allie had to bite back an impulse to tell her what she thought about Jesse Burns and his ethics. "Of course," she made herself say.

"It might not be easy to set up, either. A lot of people won't give someone like me the time of day. Do you have any suggestions of how I might approach him?"

"Well, yes, I do, actually." Excited, Allie explained about the markets and Jesse Burns' involvement. "I know that he's going to make an ad for the local TV station. I've already talked to the cameraman and reporter who will organize it because we had to decide on the things most likely to draw people to the markets. And I was thinking, Georgie—if it's okay with you, we could maybe set up a fortune teller's tent? Then I could suggest to the reporter that that would be something different, and a drawcard for the markets to film Jesse having a session with you? I mean, it would all come across as a bit of fun, but then who knows what you might find out…?" Her voice trailed off. "Does that all sound too iffy?"

"No, no." Georgie's voice was suddenly alive, interested. "I've done this sort of thing before. I've made TV ads to promote my father's RV business back home, and I've done ads to bring people to little retro trailer gatherings as well. It's a long story, and I'll tell you all about it one day! I think it's a brilliant idea, Allie. Do you think you can organize it?"

Allie felt as though a weight was lifting off her shoulders. She had so needed to take action, to do something to help, rather than just spinning her wheels and help-lessly watching Chris go further downhill.

"Let me make a few phone calls and get back to you," she said, barely able to sit still with excitement. "I believe they were planning to film the ad the day after tomorrow. And I can take care of organizing the neces-sary permissions for you to set up a tent at the markets—well, I'll find a tent, of course. All you need to do is show up with the crystal ball."

"Do it." Georgie's voice was warm, exultant. "Call me back as soon as you know."

15

Crisis Point

"You can put that down right now."

The voice behind him stopped Harrison in his tracks. He gritted his teeth, hissed out a curse, and slowly turned to face his father, dropping the ring in his right hand into his pocket first. He stared at his father challengingly, holding up the necklace in his left hand. "So." He treated his father to an unpleasant grin. "Busted."

His father looked at him as though he was lower than a cockroach. "Busted, indeed. And you can take that grin off your face. Nothing is amusing about this situation."

Harrison threw the necklace to his father, who made no move to catch it, letting it bounce off his chest and fall to the ground. "Here. Have it. It's all you think about anyway. Money, possessions, your precious family name."

"A name that I see you have no respect for whatsoever, Harrison." His father stared at him unblinkingly for a few seconds and then sighed and pinched the bridge of his nose. "This has to stop. I can't have you living in this house and stealing from your mother and your sister." He let his hand drop, and his lip curled in a sneer. "And letting your sister take the blame for what you've taken."

Harrison stared at him and felt the usual revulsion curl in his gut. Always on about getting an education, getting a good job, investments, and influence…

He didn't want to turn into his father. There was no *way* he was going to turn into his father. There were faster and easier ways to make money, to have power. "I thought you were going to Sydney today," he said sulkily. "What are you doing back here?"

"No, I let you *think* I was going to Sydney. I've suspected for a while that you were behind the things going missing." His father's lip curled. "Who else could it be but the family junkie?"

"So you set me up." Harrison jigged from one foot to another. His skin felt itchy; his blood was zinging through his veins. If he didn't take something soon, he didn't know what he would do. "Now what? Going to drag me off to the police station again?"

"I didn't drag you off there before," his father said grimly. "That was entirely your doing, being stupid enough to take drugs on a school program and causing an accident. An almost *fatal* accident. I was the one who had to go in to bail you out, remember?"

Harrison shook his head in disgust. He couldn't be bothered talking to his father anymore. "I'm going."

His father took a step to the side, blocking the door as Harrison came towards him. "Not yet."

"Old man, don't think you can stop me." Harrison itched to shove his father to the ground, but a degree of sanity prevailed. Or more likely rat cunning. He needed money, and if the well of stolen goods in his father's house was drying up, then his father himself was the only way he had of getting it. Short of holding up a convenience store or something like that.

He injected menace into his voice. "Get out of my way, dad."

"Harrison." His father's voice was tense. He was trying to sound reasonable, but the dislike came through anyway. "I want you to agree to go to rehab. We can send you away somewhere quiet, give you a chance to get past this."

"Yeah, you'd like that, wouldn't you? Get me out of the way. No more embarrassment. Well, I'm not going." He put his hand on his father's arm and pushed.

His father rocked on his feet but stayed in place. "Harrison, you're not welcome here as things are. If you don't agree to go into rehab, I don't know what's going to become of you—but I'm not going to support you in this habit anymore."

"Support me in my habit," Harrison mimicked, throwing all the sarcasm he could muster into the words. "It's not as though you can't afford it. And you *will* support me. Don't forget, daddy dear, I know a lot about your wheeling and dealing over the last few years. I kept my eyes and ears open." He rocked back on his heels and laughed at his father. "What's the saying? I know where the bodies are buried."

"So now you're blackmailing me?" Jesse snapped. "A new low, even for you."

Harrison made some quick calculations. He'd seen the flash of anger and apprehension in his father's eyes. Yeah, he did know too much. "If you're going to toss me out, I have to find somewhere to live. Unless you want it known that your son Harrison is living on the streets? You, the big man of St Georges basin?" He put out a hand and wriggled his fingers. "Give me five grand, and I'll disappear."

"Give you money." His father heaved a sigh. "And what do you plan to do with it, Harrison? Buy more drugs. You'll wind up dead of an overdose. Giving you money is *not* the answer. Give rehab a try. What have you got to lose?

"My freedom. And that's just for starters. I don't want any part of you or your solutions." He let his eyes bore into his father's. "Five grand. And I'm out of here."

His father stared at him, and Harrison could see the calculation going on behind his eyes. Finally, he spoke.

"I'm not giving you five grand, but I will give you two. It's not going to last—you haven't got the patience or the intelligence to do anything with it. But it'll give you breathing space for a week to think over my suggestion."

Harrison didn't even try to hide the triumph in his eyes. He knew which buttons to press. And a couple of grand would see him right for a few days, a few days where he could plan what else he could use against his father.

Oh yes, he knew his target. "Go and get it then, daddy. I know you keep cash in your safe. Pity I haven't worked out the combination yet."

His father held out a hand. "I'll get the money. But first, give me whatever it was you just put in your pocket. You're not stealing any more things from this house."

For a moment, Harrison debated whether to protest,

pretend his father was imagining things. But no, if he could get two grand, he could get more. His father would pay anything to protect his reputation.

He slid his hand into his pocket, got the ring, and dropped it into his father's hand. The black opal that his mother treasured so much flashed fire at him.

"Thank you. Now come with me. I'm not letting you out of my sight until you are out of this house."

His father turned on his heel and stalked out, and Harrison followed him, grinning.

Jesse stood at the expansive wall of glass in his office overlooking the beach and fought down the fury that he'd managed to control the whole time he'd been talking to his son.

Harrison was the biggest problem that he'd experienced in his life so far—and that was saying something because he'd escaped the consequences of quite a few bad decisions by the skin of his teeth. The boy had always been self-entitled, arrogant, and ignorant of what he owed his family.

There was no way he would let a boy that he didn't even *like* ruin his life.

He could pay him off, yes—and he would have done it, too, if he thought Harrison would stay away. But he'd be back with his hand out, looking for more money to top up the well every time he ran out. And he'd have something to hold over his father's head every time.

The thought of all that lay ahead made his blood run cold.

First things first. To fight your enemy, you had to know exactly where they were and what they were doing.

He picked up the phone to arrange 24/7 surveillance of his son for the next week. It came at a price that made his eyes water because it included electronic surveillance and tapping phones, and there was no way that was legal.

Luckily, Jesse had people like that on his payroll. It had paid off in the past.

Now it had come to this. His biggest threat was someone in his own family.

16

Calling in the Team

A FULL DAY and a night had passed without incident, and Georgie and Scott were able to spend a few hours in their kayaks around the beautiful waterways of St Georges Basin, without having to follow suspects or track down miscreants. This was what it was supposed to be like, Georgie thought, when they were back at the park listening to music, sitting in camp chairs outside their RV. They should be enjoying a trip around Australia, exploring the continent and making wonderful memories.

Unfortunately, that sort of thing had been all too thin on the ground since she had arrived. So, after they had done what they could to help the Moore family, she decided, they were going to just *travel* for a while. Just mindless enjoyment, watching the miles unroll under the wheels, seeing the sights.

She said as much to Scott.

Scott raised his eyebrows at her; a small smile tugging at his mouth. "I've heard that one before."

She smiled back at him. "Well, we did manage it for a few weeks. In between helping out your sisters, and coming here." She considered it for a moment. "There are always going to be more people that need help. Always someone in a crisis. We can't help everybody. So let's take some time for ourselves."

"True." Scott stared at the sky, propping his feet up on a footstool, basking in the sun like a lazy lion. "But when you think about it: emergency services, therapists, priests, counsellors… people like that see people in crisis all the time, and they know they can't help everybody, but they do what they can." He turned his warm gaze on Georgie. "And you, my Georgie, are the same. If someone needs your help, and you *know* they need your help, you're not going to turn them away."

She ran her fingers down his arm, and then linked her fingers with his. "You're right, of course. But a girl can hope, can't she?"

"Indeed she can." He gave her hand a squeeze. "But when you look at people like Chris and Allie Moore, you've got to admit that it's worth taking a week or so out of seeing the sights around the country to help them get their lives back on track."

"Yes," said Georgie, "it is."

"When are you scheduled to do the TV slot with Jesse Burns?"

"About eleven tomorrow morning, at Hyams Beach. His own backyard, so to speak." Georgie drummed her fingers on the arm of the chair, thinking about it. "The film crew are catching up with some of the local farmers about their produce, and they're also planning to film an interview with a craft store owner from Huskisson.

Showing different parts of the region, I think that's the idea. Bringing people to St Georges Basin. The camera crew suggested we meet up on the beach." She turned amused eyes on Scott. "They want me in a long flowing skirt, walking barefoot along the beach, Gypsy bangles jangling." She laughed. "Looks like a tank top and shorts are not going to cut it."

"Of course not," said Scott. "Eighth generation gypsy and all. You should be wearing one of Rosa's embroidered shawls."

At his words, a pang of homesickness went through Georgie, shocking her with its sharpness. She missed Great-Grandma Rosa, and her father, and her brother Jerry and his fiancee Tammy. She was loving seeing Australia with Scott, but it had been a while since she'd seen anyone from home.

Able to read her well as always, Scott leaned over and kissed her on the cheek. "Missing them all, are you?"

"Of course." She waved his concern away. "But you were in the US for over a year. I've only been here a few months. You must have missed your family too."

"I did." He squeezed her hand. "But then I met this mysterious American gypsy, and suddenly I had a very good reason to stay in the US of A."

"Anyway." Georgie's thoughts returned to her meeting with Jesse. "Back to the TV segment: they want to film Jesse walking along the beach and then meeting me, and something about seeing his future… I think the idea is to segue from Jesse's future to the future of the area. Load of rubbish really, but I can see how it might appeal to the viewers. And then we apparently go and find a rock to sit on and they're going to stage it so that you can see the blue sky and the waves through the crystal ball, some arty shot, and then they're going to get close-ups of me telling Jesse what I can see in the crystal ball. And then they're going to suggest people come and see me at the inaugural seasonal markets."

"And you're doing this tomorrow."

"Yes, tomorrow." Thinking about it, Georgie felt a strange shift in her body, a sort of knowing. Past and future future were strange things, when it came to telling fortunes. She was certain in her own mind that every-thing was all laid out, somewhere; some huge tapestry, with the threads weaving in and out of the past and future.

This meeting with Jesse Burns was going to be signif-icant. She knew it.

If there was one thing that Georgie had learned while using the crystal ball to help solve other people's prob-lems, it was that things tended to work out better if you didn't leave it *all* up to the crystal ball.

That being so, before the scheduled meeting with Jesse Burns, it would make sense to find out as much about him as possible.

And who else to do that, but Bluey?

She knew Scott's brother well enough now not to have to go through Scott first. She brought up his number on her phone and called.

Bluey's voice, so much like Scott's but with a slightly harsher undertone, answered her right away. "Well if it isn't my favorite gypsy fortune teller. Hey there, Georgie.

What can I do for you?" There was a slightly wry tone to his last five words.

"What can you do for me?" Georgie laughed. "Couldn't I be ringing up just for a chat? Shoot the breeze?"

"You could," Bluey admitted, "but it's not likely, in the middle of a working day. I've been expecting a call from you, anyway."

Momentarily diverted, Georgie felt her eyebrows fly up. "You have? Why?"

"Oh, just because it's been a while. I figured you couldn't roam around the countryside for too much longer without finding some trouble to get into. Am I right or am I right?"

Georgie grinned at the phone. "Yeah, you're right. But we will eventually make our way across the country to see you, Bluey. And then it really *will* be social."

Blue snorted. "I guess we'll see about that, given the way trouble follows you around. Anyway, I'll be happy to see you, whatever the reason. Do you know how long it's been since I've caught up with my brother?"

"Yes," Georgie said. "He was talking about you just the other night; he figures it's something like a month shy of two years. That sound about right?"

"Pretty much. Well, well. Don't tell me little bro is missing me?"

"Something like that," Georgie said with another laugh. "And I'm dying to meet you too, of course. I've met everyone else in the family. Just not our friendly neighborhood—"

Bluey's voice broke in before she could finish the sentence and say *"hacker."* Smoothly, he interjected, "... friendly neighborhood computer expert. What would you guys do without someone who knew his way around a computer?" His voice faded as he something to someone in the room with him, and then she heard the buzz of more voices in the background.

"You still there, Georgie?"

"Bad timing, Bluey? If you're busy, this can wait till later."

"It's cool. But I'll ring you back on another phone, okay? Give me a couple of minutes."

"Sure."

Georgie waited, and true to his word, Bluey called back a few moments later. "Sorry about that, Georgie." He lowered his voice. "Not sure, but that phone might have been compromised."

"Is it better if I send you an email or something first?"

"No, this number should be fine. Delete the other one. This is something that's come up just in the last couple of days. Anyway…what's the problem?"

Georgie gave him a potted history of what she and Scott had been up to, the plight faced by the Moores, and the information she had so far. "Not much to go on, I know," she said. "But I thought if you could just see what you can turn up on Jesse Burns, I'll know what I'm dealing with before I meet up with him. Does that sound do-able?"

"Next time, give me something *hard*. I'll call you back later this afternoon, okay? Or it could be tonight. When did you say you're meeting up with this guy?"

"Tomorrow, about eleven. Is that giving you enough time?"

"Absolutely. Ordinarily I'd probably be able to get

you something in a couple of hours, but there's something here I have to attend to first."

"Like a phone that is not secure?"

"That, and a few other things. Gotta go. Give my regards to little bro." With that, Bluey was gone.

17

Filming

WALKING along the water's edge at Hyam's Beach, sandals in one hand, Georgie felt a sense of déjà vu. Over the years, she'd participated in quite a few ads for Johnny B. Goode's RV Empire, and she'd made a few more for her little band of retro travelers in the USA.

Cameramen all seemed to want the same type of thing: *Go down there, walk towards me but not too fast, look out to sea, stop and dip your toes in the water... then we'll have Jesse Burns walk along towards you, right, and you'll greet each other. We'll have some nice shots of Hyam's Beach and even pan up to Jesse's house...*

They had a couple of goes at it, and she saw that Jesse Burns was just as comfortable in front of the cameras as she was. Probably more so: she had a feeling that he would have spent a great deal of his life opening things, donating money, sponsoring things, being seen at black-tie events, and so on. He'd have made a great politician. She was a bit surprised that he hadn't already made a run for Parliament.

They did half a dozen takes until the cameraman

was satisfied, and then he futzed around a bit more, getting Georgie to stare out to sea thoughtfully, and then up to the heavens as though she was tapping into the great beyond.

Cheesy, Georgie acknowledged, but in a strange way not so far from reality.

The cameraman and his sidekick huddled together to watch the playback, then the cameraman moved his headphones away from his ear and nodded at her, giving her a thumbs up. "Nice work. This is going to look good. Now, if we can get you and Mr. Burns to move over here—" he indicated the natural rock formation where he'd set up Georgie's crystal ball "— we'll do the next take. I'll get a few shots of you looking into the crystal ball. Let me see—" He turned around and looked to where the sun was. "Yes, that'll do it. I can get a few shots of the sea and sky through the crystal ball."

"Okay." Georgie looked over to where Scott was unwrapping her crystal ball and then setting it on the same worn piece of velvet that Rosa had used for years. He knew how much she treasured it, and there was no way he was going to let anything happen to it.

As she followed the cameraman across to the rocks, Jesse Burns fell into step beside her.

"You're not what I expected," he said.

Georgie turned her head to look at him and raised her eyebrows. "Really? What *were* you expecting? Full Gypsy regalia? Maybe a gypsy wagon?"

He laughed, a rich deep laugh that made him sound genial and approachable. After getting Bluey's report the night before, she knew that the real Jesse Burns was no such thing; she was seeing his public persona.

Well, she could play along with this.

Georgie looked down at her filmy white skirt, and the bright cotton embroidered scarf she had draped around the tank top she wore. The outfit would have been at home on any beach without the scarf, but it added just the right touch. She'd arranged her hair in loose looping braids and had added a couple of dangling earrings for effect.

See, Mr. Burns, she said silently. *You're not the only one who knows how to project an image.*

He put a hand on her arm to slow her down. "So tell me," he said in a low voice, deliberately lagging behind the cameraman. "Is this stuff for real, or is it a show? Like those illusionists in Vegas?"

Georgie turned her head to meet his eyes. She kept a smile on her face but made sure the smile was in her eyes too. She wanted Jesse to trust her—right up until the time she could bring him down. "I really am an eighth-generation Gypsy, Mr. Burns. My great-grand-mother owned this crystal ball before me, and what she can do puts me in the shade."

Will his eyes sharpened, and he gave her a quick nod. "Okay, I get it that you have a gypsy heritage, but you didn't answer my question. Is this stuff for real?"

"There are plenty of people that have told me so," she said. "But why don't you wait and see? I'll do a reading for you, and you can make your own decision."

"Suitably vague," he said. "But I believe that's how it's often played. All right, then. What sorts of things are we going to be looking at?" He kept his voice casual, but Georgie was attuned to him now, and it wasn't hard to sense the underlying caution. This was a man with a lot to hide; he certainly wouldn't want some of the deals he'd been involved in exposed in a TV interview that thousands and thousands of people would see.

She tapped him playfully on the arm. "Don't worry, Mr. Burns. I *never* embarrass my clients. It'll be easy enough for you to shut me down if you think I'm venturing into territory you don't want to be made public."

That made him stop in his tracks. He turned to face her, glancing again at the cameraman first to make sure he wasn't in earshot. "Is there likely to be a *reason* I would want to shut you down?" He squinted at her in the bright sun. The cameraman had made them take their sunglasses off, the better to see their faces. "Because I don't take kindly to being set up."

Oh, yes, he has something to hide, all right. Georgie shook her head. "Mr. Burns—"

"Call me Jesse," he said with a hint of impatience. "I've told you that."

"Jesse, then." Georgie regarded him seriously. "When I read a crystal ball, I do sometimes see… shall we say, sensitive information. If I do, I don't disclose it publicly, especially in a TV interview. I know this aims to attract people to the area, so I'll play to the crowd, give them what they want. Don't worry; you'll come out of it looking good."

He glanced over to where the cameraman was giving them hurry-up motions, looking at his watch. "And if there is any… sensitive… information, are you going to pass that on, or not?"

Georgie was instantly reminded of how Drew had asked virtually the same question a few nights ago.

"That's up to you. I'll give you the opportunity to hear it privately if you wish."

"At a cost, no doubt." He smiled to take the sting out of his words, but Georgie just smiled back and shook her head.

Jesse gave her the kind of look that meant he was reconsidering his first impression of her. Georgie took care to keep her face open, friendly, and approachable. Sure, she wanted him to respect her and respect what she did, but there was no need to send a signal that she could be dangerous to him.

The cameraman patted the flat rock on which he'd placed the crystal ball, with room for Georgie to sit beside it. He'd spread the towel that Scott got out of the car on the sand beside it and told Jesse to sit there, so the camera crew could get shots of him gazing up at Georgie, getting her reactions, with the crystal ball neatly between the two of them.

"Okay," said the cameraman, once he was satisfied that he had them where he wanted, with the sun in the right position. "Let's test the sound. Georgie, can you just say a few words?"

"My name is Georgie Goode," Georgie said. She had been through this so many times she was on autopilot. "I'm delighted to be giving Jesse Burns a reading today. Mr. Burns is an active person in the local community, and I'm sure he's going to enjoy this as much as I am." She gave a big smile right into the camera. "I hope to see many of you along to the markets on Saturday."

"Nice. That'll do. Now you, Jesse."

"My name is Jesse Burns," said Jesse with a grin at the same camera that Georgie had just targeted. "I'm excited about this, the inaugural seasonal markets to take place at Sussex Inlet. As you can see, I'm at the beautiful beach near my home, here at Hyams beach, but the whole area is filled with beautiful waterways and lovely spots to picnic. It's also filled with—"

"Okay, good," the cameraman interrupted. "That'll do it. We'll do the intro later." He moved the tripod slightly and adjusted the camera again. "That's better. We're ready to roll. Just do what you normally do, Georgie. In the end, we might have Jesse ask you a few questions, get you to give more answers… That kind of thing. Okay with that?"

"Fine," Georgie said.

Jesse Burns echoed her sentiments, and they got underway.

Georgie went into her usual spiel at the beginning, about guaranteeing nothing and about how she was sometimes just as surprised as her clients and what she was able to see, and then smiled at Jesse. "Sometimes, I just sit here and look into the crystal ball and see what comes up. Sometimes my clients ask me questions. How would you like to approach this?"

Jesse looked at her challengingly. "If I ask you a question, wouldn't that give you a bit of a heads-up as to what I'm interested in? Wouldn't it be better just to let you run with this?"

Georgie smiled back at him sweetly. "Whatever you like. I'm happy just to get started and see what we can find out."

Ignoring the camera crew, she closed her eyes for a moment and ran her fingertips gently over the crystal ball. She was aware of Scott, not far away, supporting her as always in anything she did. She let her attention drift away and felt the crystal ball grow warmer under her hands. Scott had kept it covered, and in a cooler bag so it didn't get too hot in the sun while filming the initial walk down the beach, and she could already feel a different definite difference in the temperature.

Slowly, she smoothed her hand her cupped hands down over the sides of the crystal ball and let them rest gently on the lower half of the globe.

Bright and clear, the crystal ball blinked back at her.

Darn. Was it going to be one of those days? Surely she wasn't going to have to say, "Sorry, it seems the universe doesn't have anything to tell me today."

That wouldn't do much to bring the crowds in.

"Am I supposed to be saying anything?" Jesse asked, peering at it. "Or am I supposed to be *seeing* anything?" He winked at the camera. "Nothing mysterious here, folks!"

Despite herself, Georgie felt a frisson of annoyance. Couldn't the man be generous enough to know that he was doing this as an ad to bring people to his area? To his town? No, Jesse Burns was one of those people who thought it was always about him.

"Cut." The cameraman put his hand briefly in front of the camera lens and took it away again. Georgie knew from her previous experience with this that that was a signal to him when new footage started.

He looked at Jesse. "Mr. Burns, it's probably best if we keep this positive, as an ad for the markets."

"No," Georgie said, tilting her head to look up at the cameraman. "Let it go. It would be best if you showed it like it is. Don't worry, this sometimes happens initially, but it's rare for me not to get anything. We'll just keep going, let people see what the real experience is like." This time, she couldn't help herself: she had to shoot Jesse a challenging look.

Jesse clearly didn't like being reprimanded. "Alright,

let's go again." He looked at his watch. "I do have a meeting to get to in about half an hour, so it'd be good if we could wrap this up soon."

I'll wrap you up all right, thought Georgie. *And it'll be my pleasure to do it.*

18

More to Know

ALTHOUGH HE DIDN'T HAVE a specific question, Georgie had a good idea of what Jesse Burns might want to know. Thanks to Bluey, she knew Burns had a deal pending worth hundreds of millions: a mega-development in one of Sydney's popular suburbs. She also knew that Jesse had already been notified, through clandestine channels, that it should get the green light today.

The development hadn't been popular, with people protesting against the plan because of heritage listings. However, Jesse had a few politicians in his pocket and also had managed to bury his interests several levels deep in shell companies.

She gave a mental sigh. Politics, power, corrupt deals that would make people obscenely rich. How many times was she going to encounter this?

Fortunately, Bluey loved a challenge. It had taken him longer than he expected to dig up information, but he'd come good in time for the reading.

Georgie knew that Scott's brother had his own code of ethics. If someone deserved to be taken down, he wouldn't hesitate. Unless, she surmised, it was contrary to the interests of some long game he was playing.

She passed her fingers over the crystal ball again, opening herself up to whatever the messages might be. She knew that she wouldn't necessarily see anything, but she'd hoped that today she would, with the cameras recording everything.

She looked at the crystal ball again. Still, nothing. Then she gradually became aware that this time, she was receiving information differently.

Images, words, sensations were coming together and merging into definite impressions.

Oh yes, Jesse Burns was on tenterhooks. He desperately needed his big investment to go through without anyone being the wiser that he was at the helm. That was probably why he was antsy today: he was waiting for the big news.

There was nothing she would have liked better than to expose him to the world, but that was going to come soon enough without her intervention. Right now, she needed to focus on her immediate problem: a wonderful little family here at Sussex Inlet whose livelihood had been destroyed by this man.

Jesse himself interrupted her thoughts again. "Are you seeing anything yet?" She heard the faint note of disdain in his voice and disliked him even more if that were possible. Masking her true feelings, she looked up at him with a small smile. "Yes. I'm getting quite a lot, actually—don't be misled by the fact that you can't see anything in the crystal ball. It's possible, but sometimes, the information is for me only."

Jesse let out one of his jolly laughs, projecting the image of a staunch local supporter who was happy to go along with the facade that she was putting up for the sake of the markets. "And tell me, what do you see?"

Georgie ignored the larger question that he had in his mind and opened her mind to smaller things, things you could reveal in front of the intrusive eye of a TV camera. She pictured Jesse Burns' body and organs, opening up her mind to his general state of health. That usually revealed something; most people had something wrong with them or some injury in the past.

Sure enough, an image flashed into her mind of a small blonde-haired boy, about eight or nine years old, hopping along on crutches. His right ankle was in plaster.

Her eyes met his. "When you were a boy—I'm guessing, maybe eight or nine—you had an accident. Judging by the plaster, I think either a broken leg, a broken ankle? Something like that. I see you on crutches, and that leg still pains you." She nodded, glancing at his tanned leg in designer shorts. "Your right leg."

At last, a spark of interest entered Jesse's eyes. "Yes, you're right. I did break my ankle as a kid. Skate-boarding accident."

Satisfied that she had snared him now, Georgie nodded.

More images flooded in. She focused on Jesse's children, his family. "You have three children. Two boys and a girl."

Jesse shook a finger at her. "True, true. But that information is everywhere. Now, Georgie, if we want people to come along and see you and find out things they can't find out from anyone else, you need to give me more than that." Staring straight at the camera, he hammed it up a bit, raising and lowering his eyebrows a couple of times, then flashed the beaming, trademark Jesse Burns smile. The smile said *I'm just kidding around*, but Georgie could feel his underlying impatience. Despite the information about his childhood accident, he was still skeptical.

Under her fingers, the crystal ball grew warmer still. She glanced down and was satisfied to see the familiar soft grey-white mist forming in the center.

Jesse's eyes followed hers, and she heard an intake of breath. "Well, look at that. The crystal ball is turning cloudy inside. What does that mean?"

"Sometimes it means that images will start to appear; sometimes it just stays that way, and anything I see is in my mind only."

Jesse stared hard at the crystal ball. "Okay. So, what else can you see?"

This time, unbidden, an image floated into Georgie's mind of a sleek-looking woman with artfully streaked blonde hair, dressed in expensive casual clothes, with a butterfly-shaped pendant suspended from a thin gold chain. The crystal ball still showed nothing, but the image in Georgie's mind was as clear as a photograph. Certain that the woman was Jesse's wife, she said: "Your wife has a beautiful pendant. It's in the shape of a butterfly, studded with what looks like rubies and diamonds; a very nice piece." More information flooded her mind. She looked up at Jesse again. "No, she *had* it… she doesn't own it anymore?"

Jesse's eyes narrowed just a little. He kept the smile on his face and nodded. "Unfortunately, my wife lost that pendant earlier this year."

"She was upset, I think." Georgie closed her eyes

and could see Jesse's wife's face. Her expression betrayed annoyance and loss. Instinctively, Georgie knew that the pendant meant a great deal to her.

"If your crystal ball could tell us where that pendant is, I'm sure Jenna would be eternally grateful to you," Jesse said with a concerned look on his face, totally manufactured for the camera. "It's been handed down through the family, and apart from being quite valuable, it has a lot of sentimental value."

Another image came into Georgie's mind. This time, the picture was of a shed or old garage. She did see a shadowy entrance, and in the dimness beyond some machines… she concentrated, but instead of growing sharper, the image dimmed, and she couldn't see what was inside the garage at all. But then the image pulled back, enough for her to see shrubs and trees around the shed, as though a camera was taking a wider view. Behind the trees, she saw the exterior of a house.

A *blue* house.

You didn't have to be a genius to join the dots. It was Chad Royston's house. If the pendant wasn't there, it certainly had been… and she had a fair idea who would have taken it there.

She looked at Jesse and decided to give him part of the information, but not enough to go charging off to confront Chad. "I see a garage. Whether the pendant is there, or it once was there, I don't know."

"A garage?" Jesse's brow furrowed. "You mean, might Jenna have dropped it in the garage at home? When she was getting out of the car?"

Georgie was certain that the garage adjoining Jesse Burns' million-dollar home would not be remotely like the one at Chad Royston's place, but she kept that to herself as well. "I'm not getting information that specific, but I feel that you would have noticed it if it was in your garage at home. No, I think this is somewhere else." She shrugged. "Perhaps you should think about where you and your wife have been, whether it might be at a friend's house—or even in a different city."

Jesse looked as though he was going to say something else but closed his mouth again. An image of Harrison floated into Georgie's mind, and she knew that Jesse thought the same as she did: that Harrison was behind the disappearance of the pendant. He had most likely taken it to a garage in a backyard somewhere to sell it on.

She decided to push a little. Thanks to Bluey, she knew the timeline of a few things that Jesse had going. "One more thing: I have a strong feeling that you're going to get a phone call sometime today, with news that you've been waiting for. It concerns a major development that you have in the pipeline."

She felt the instant tension in Jesse's body. It was almost a surge of panic, but he covered it with a laugh. "Well, that's good to know. I'll be waiting on that phone call. I've got quite a few things on the go at any one time, being in real estate development. It could be any one of several things. And some of them will bring jobs to the local area." He waited for a beat and then drew back, looking up at the cameraman and tapping his watch. "Sorry guys, but I need to go. Have you got enough to work with?"

"And cut." The cameraman slid his earphones back off back around his neck again. "We just have a couple of staging shots to do, Mr. Burns. It won't take long, and then we can let you go." He looked at Georgie. "That was interesting stuff about the broken leg and the missing pendant. Should be enough to bring people along to your tent at the markets."

"I hope so." Georgie glanced back at the crystal ball again. The mist was dissipating.

She was glad that nothing too definite had appeared there today. It looked like the universe was cooperating in her efforts to bring down Harrison and his father.

Five minutes later, it was all over. She chatted briefly to the cameraman, who predictably was interested enough to ask more questions, and then Jesse took his leave and strode away.

But not before agreeing that he would return to Georgie's tent at the markets for a follow-up piece.

Georgie was happy enough with that. By the weekend, she felt that a lot more of the puzzle would be in place.

19

Harrison in Trouble

HARRISON MIGHT HAVE BEEN ORDERED to leave, but they could hardly stop him from taking his things. Buzzing with anger, he grabbed a large duffel bag from the store-room of the garage and tossed it on his bed. He crammed in shorts, jeans, T-shirts, and underwear until the bag bulged and then shoved his iPad and charger on top of them.

He couldn't wait to be out of this place. He'd miss the meals —his mother was an excellent cook—but he could do without the nagging and long-suffering looks from both his mother and sister.

He glanced around his room and wondered how difficult it would be to remove the wall-mounted TV. Probably too much trouble to get it off now, but he could come back for it. He still had a key, and unless they changed the locks, he would be able to come and go as he pleased when they were out.

He heard a sound behind him and turned to see his mother standing in the doorway. There was no sign of friendliness on her face.

"So. You're going, then."

"Didn't have a choice, did I?" His glance raked her, and he curled his lip, knowing that that would press a few buttons.

Sure enough, her lips tightened, and she folded her arms, leaning against the doorjamb. "You have only yourself to blame for this, Harrison. God knows, your father and I have done nothing but try to help you over the years. But ever since you took up with that Tyler—"

"Spare me, will you? I'm going; you don't need to go on at me anymore." With one hard yank, he zipped up the bag and slung it over his shoulder. "I'll be back later for a few more of my things." He went to push past her, but she stayed in place, her eyes glittering with anger.

"What have you done with all the jewelry you stole from me, Tyler? And don't blame your sister. Leah might have borrowed it sometimes without permission, but she always returned it."

"Yeah, of course, it's me. It's always me. You don't think for a minute that your precious Leah might've worn it out and *lost* it. It's too convenient to blame the black sheep of the family, right?"

"Stop it." She hissed out the words with surprising venom. "Just stop it, Harrison. You're a user and a liar. I know your father told you that he hired a private investigator, so we know exactly what you've been up to and who you've been seeing."

"Oh, you do, do you?" He shifted the bag to the other shoulder, grinning at her without any humor at all. "I bet you didn't see me going into any pawnshop with your jewelry, though, did you?"

"Oh, I'm quite convinced you've got the contacts to ensure you don't have to do that." Her chin came up, and she stared at him challengingly. "You're becoming a very gifted little criminal."

"Why don't you tell me what you really think?"

"You won't be coming back here unless you're prepared to go into rehab."

"Well, mother dear, I'm not going into rehab, so I won't be back here, will I?"

"Harrison." She put a hand on his elbow as he brushed past. "Please, just tell me where the butterfly pendant is. That's the one piece I care about."

Relishing the pain he saw in her eyes, Harrison just let his grin grow wider. "What butterfly pendant? I have no idea what you're talking about." He held her gaze just long enough so that she would know, without any doubt, that he was perfectly well aware of where it was.

"I'll buy it back." She almost spat out the words, but Harrison was unmoved.

"Much as I need the money, seeing as how you've cut me off, I'm afraid I can't help you there. Maybe you can hire another private investigator to see if he can find it. Good luck with that."

Leaving her behind, he clattered down the stairs and through the foyer, taking the time to give his sister the finger as he passed the living room. She glared at him and called out, "Good riddance!"

Harrison jogged down the front steps and around to the garage.

His mother's car was where it always was, in the carport next to the garage. Humming to himself, he pressed the key fob button that unlocked the Prius, her pride and joy, and slid in behind the driver's seat. Wasting no time, he fired it up and headed out of the driveway.

As he had expected, she came flying out of the front door, down the steps, and out of the gate to stare after him as he rocketed off down the street. In the rearview mirror, he saw her plant her hands on her hips before she shook her fist at him and turned to go back inside.

Mission accomplished.

She'd probably guess he'd gone to Tyler's—where else did he have to go? But she could come and get her damn car herself. No doubt daddy dear would drive her later today.

An idea came to him, and he grinned.

If that is, he hadn't sold it first.

***

Harrison wasn't expecting what he walked into when he arrived at Tyler's. He parked the Prius behind Tyler's five-year-old 4WD and walked around to the apartment that Tyler had claimed for his own at the back of the garage. He pushed open the door before realizing that someone else was there.

Hard hands grabbed him, and before he had time to do more than let out a startled yelp, he found his arms twisted behind his back.

A few paces away, Tyler lay on the floor in a fetal position, protecting his head with his hands, his knees jammed tightly up to his chest as far as he could get them. He was moaning.

Oh, shit.

"Hey, man," Harrison said hastily, struggling. "This has got nothing to do with me. He—

"Just shut up." The man who held him slammed a fist into the side of his head, and Harrison went down like a ton of bricks. He tried to scuttle away but copped a hard shoe to the midsection before he could get out of range.

"Now, isn't this fortuitous." A quiet, well-spoken voice sounded from across the room.

Harrison squeezed his eyes shut tight and groaned. *Not him.*

This was turning out to be a shitty day.

The voice from across the room went on. "We came to collect from your friend Tyler, but it appears he has no money. You, on the other hand, owe us money too. We'll be happy to collect from you instead."

Wincing at the pain, Harrison pushed himself up to where he could lean against the lounge. He tried for a conciliatory tone. "Listen, mate; I told you I'd get you the money. Don't I always?"

"No, you don't always. And we are beginning to doubt that you're going to come good with it, aren't we, Bruno?"

The other man grunted in agreement.

"I've spoken to my father," Harrison improvised hastily, drawing on the conversation he'd had with his father the day before. "He said he'd only help me out this one last time if I agree to go into rehab." He went to shake his head helplessly, but the movement brought pain glancing through his head, and for a moment, the world went dark. Bruno had one hell of a punch on him.

The man he knew as Wally just laughed. "*You* go to rehab? That's a good one. And did you agree?"

"Yes," Harrison lied. "If it's the only way to get you guys off my back, sure, I agreed. Go to rehab for a month or two, come out, and soon I'll be back running my own life again." He let his head sink into his hands. "Oh, my head."

"Take a look at your friend Tyler, and consider yourself lucky that it's only your head." He heard footsteps approaching and glanced up fearfully. The man just looked down at him with an assessing gleam in his eye. "What are the terms of this agreement you have with your father? He gives you the money so you can pay me off? If I were him, I'd hardly agree to that. Not knowing you as I do."

Harrison knew that he had no chance of keeping the two grand that his father had given him. *Give it up now; live to fight another day.* He swallowed hard and said, "I told him I'd have to give you something, or I wouldn't make it to rehab. He would only give me two grand."

"Two grand." Wally's voice held no emotion at all. "And the rest?"

"You tell me when, where and how you want it delivered, and I pass that on to him," Harrison lied. "He'll send somebody he can trust with the money."

"And what guarantee do we have that this will happen if I accept the two grand as a down payment?"

Harrison looked up and let out an almost genuine laugh. "Come on; you know who my old man is. Mr. Clean of Hyams Beach? The one who sits on boards all over Sydney? Do you think there's any way in the world he wants this getting out? Don't worry; he'll pay up. It's chump change for him."

Wally extended a hand. "Give me the two grand."

Harrison nodded over at the duffel bag. "It's in there. Side pocket."

Wally nodded in Bruno's direction. The other man lifted the bag, tossed it on the lounge that Harrison was leaning against, and rummaged in the side pocket. He fished around a bit and then came up with the money, secured by a rubber band. Expressionlessly, he flicked through the cash, counting. He nodded. "All here."

"I want the money tomorrow," Wally said. "I'll text you the details of the meet. It won't be us picking it up, so don't get smart."

"And if we are not happy," Bruno added with a grin, "we'll be sure to let you know."

Without another word, they left.

Harrison slumped against the lounge and let out a long groan. "I'm dead. I am so dead."

Across the room on the floor, Tyler didn't answer. His moans were growing quieter until finally, he just emitted a huge sigh. At length, he sat up, slowly and painfully, and Harrison's eyes widened at the sight of his face. "Oh, shit, man. They did you over."

Tyler, too sore to move, just propped himself up on the other end of the lounge and closed his eyes.

20

Going Ballistic

THE MORE HARRISON thought about the situation he was in, the madder he got. Nothing had gone right in his life since that stupid kayaking camp last year. And it *should* have been different. Just look at all he and Tyler had learned about scuba diving while they were overseas.

He, Harrison, had a gift for it; the guy running it had told him that. Not everyone picked it up as quickly as he had—in an aside, the guy had said quietly that just between them, even Tyler wasn't as good as Harrison.

He could have made the business work, he was sure of it. He had watched everything the guy running the courses overseas had done, and it was easy. Get your boat license, get the scuba licenses, do a bit of health and safety stuff… there were always people coming to St Georges Basin wanting to be shown the wonders of the deep. If only his father had agreed to bankroll him, he could've used some of the money to clear his drugs debt and then had plenty left to get something started.

Now, everything had gone to shit. His father had

kicked him out of the house, his mother had come and taken her car back, and now he had to find more money to pay off the people who beat up Tyler.

Sitting outside Tyler's house in his friend's 4WD, Harrison considered his options. He could do a runner. He had enough friends in Sydney to go and hide out for a while—but how long? Half the kids he used to go to school with were going to uni, working for their parents, or employed in some other cushy job.

And then there was the cash flow problem. He had no money to survive on.

Getting angrier by the minute, Harrison thumped the steering wheel. He didn't even have the two grand his father had given him to buy anything to take the edge off.

Not even enough money to put fuel in the car.

He could sneak back into his parents' house at night, see what he could take. He mused over that idea for a while and then shook his head. His father would be on the alert now. He wouldn't put it past him to have more cameras or alarms rigged.

Well, if none of that was going to work, where else could he get money?

His mind roved over the names of people he knew at Hyam's Beach, and other people who lived at Huskisson. He could probably sneak around at night, steal enough stuff... But it wouldn't tide him over for long.

Again, his mind went to the two men who had taken his last two grand. They'd suggested a couple of times now that he could work for them and use his influence with kids he knew from school to get them into the drug scene.

His eyes flicked up to the rear vision mirror, and he studied the cars parked in Tyler's Street. He recognized a few of them, but there were still a couple that he didn't know. More than likely, one of them hid his father's private investigator.

He closed his eyes and again felt the need for something. He had planned to either get drugs from Tyler or to use part of the two K to go out and buy.

Chris Moore. Drew Moore. Jason Hoy. Chad Royston. One by one, he ticked off the list of people who had brought him to this. They all deserved to pay in some way.

Well, he was no dummy. He'd drive around for a while until he was sure that he was not being followed. Then, he'd pay a visit to Chad's place, demand something in return for his silence. If he wasn't there, he'd move on to the Moores' place, find something to turn into cash.

And if they weren't home, he'd leave his calling card. The thought of it made him grin.

Harrison leaned forward and started the car, then took off up the street. He drove through Booderee National Park, heading back to Sussex Inlet. All the time, he watched his rear vision mirror. There was a car visible briefly, but then it turned off along the Huskisson Road. There was nobody else behind him that he could see.

Satisfied, he planted his foot on the accelerator, heading for Sussex Inlet.

On impulse, he went first to the pub. Not the fancy one where the tourists liked to hang out, but the one where Jason worked. He wandered in, caught his eye straight away, and sat down at the bar.

Jason messed about for a bit with wiping glasses, and

then served someone else, and then finally came up to him, his brows drawn together. He didn't look pleased to see him.

"What can I get you, mate?" he said, wiping a cloth over the bar in front of Harrison.

Harrison took a sneaky look around, but nobody was watching them. "Just water," he said. "Unless you want to shout me a drink."

Jason's face closed up. "You telling me you've got no money?"

"Not right this minute," Harrison said, smiling as though we didn't have a care in the world. "Just paid a debt or two, you know? Now I'm good. In the clear." Another quick look around showed that the only people in the pub were watching a horse race on TV, so he leaned forward a little. "You couldn't stake me something until tomorrow, could you? I'm good for it."

Jason heaved an impatient sigh and then went to the taps to pull him a beer. He set it down in front of Harrison and said a low voice, "Here. I'll pay for it out of my pocket, and that's the only credit you're getting here today. Okay?"

Harrison quelled the urge to jump across the counter and grab Jason by his grimy collar. "Come on, man. Just until tomorrow."

Jason shook his head and then turned to fiddle with a couple of bottles on the shelf—bottles that didn't need rearranging, as far as Harrison could tell. At length, Jason glanced around to ensure that nobody was in hearing range and then turned back to Harrison. He was close enough so that he couldn't be overheard, but not so close that it looked as though he was telling secrets. Or selling drugs.

"No more credit for you, sorry. And if I were you, I'd watch out: the word is out that the heavies are down from Sydney, asking questions. When you finish that beer, nick off." He tossed a packet of chips from under the counter in front of Harrison and then disappeared through a doorway to a back room.

Glaring after him, Jason drank half the beer in three large swallows and then set the glass down. He waited until Jason emerged again and then said casually, "Chad gave me a printout, this stuff about how I can start training. He wouldn't be home now, would he?"

Jason looked alarmed. "I wouldn't go near him if I were you, mate." Again, he wiped the counter, an excuse to stay near Harrison. "I *told* you what he said about coppers from Sydney. Stay away."

Harrison grinned triumphantly. "Why? He told me he didn't do any of that stuff now. Changed his mind, has he?"

"He's not there. Gone over to Husky to do a private training session." He hesitated. "I hear a new bloke is dealing up Culburra way. You might want to go there; try asking around."

Harrison drank the rest of his beer and set the glass down with a thump. He had no intention of going anywhere near Culburra, but it was okay with him if that's where Jason thought he was going. "You reckon I got a chance there?"

"I reckon. I hear he's trying to break in. Name's Snake."

Harrison laughed out loud. "Snake? Really?"

Jason shrugged, picked up Harrison's empty glass, and walked off down the other end of the counter. He'd finished talking.

Well, that suited Harrison. If Chad was in Huskisson, that meant there was nobody home.

He'd see what he could find.

Half an hour later, Jesse Burns was buzzed by his secretary. He had a perfectly good home office, but he liked to maintain a presence in the town—and there were certain people he didn't want anywhere near his home.

Besides, it was surprising how much you heard when you had an office in the midst of things.

He was in the middle of a Skype session with a friend in Sydney, sharing screens and looking at data, and wasn't in the mood to be interrupted.

"Just a minute," he said to his business acquaintance. Depressing the button on his phone, he said testily: "Dee, I can't take any calls right now. I told you that."

"I'm sorry, Mr. Burns. He said it was important and to tell you it was Hector calling. That you would take his call." Her voice was nervous, which meant that he had probably been snapping at her a bit too much lately. Jesse sighed. "Just a minute."

He returned to his Skype session.

"Sorry, Stephen. It sounds like it's something urgent. Wait five minutes, and if I can't keep going with this, can we reschedule for tonight?"

"No problem." The man on his screen smiled at him politely. No, of course he wouldn't object; he was going to get too much out of this sweet deal.

Jesse ended the session and pushed the button on his phone again. "Hector?"

"You've got a problem. Our subject has been…."

"Okay, hold it there." Jesse preferred not to have anything over the phone that he might not want to be made public. "I'll call you back."

He pulled out a different phone and pressed speed dial. A moment later, Hector answered. "Okay."

"What seems to be the problem?"

"Your boy's going nuts. We followed him to a pub at Sussex, watched him talk to Jason Hoy and have a drink, and when he came out, he took off up the road to the place he went to yesterday. Chad Royston. Know him?"

"I know *of* him." Jesse knew was that it was more than likely that the drugs that Harrison had obtained from Jason Hoy had come from Chad Royston, but nobody was talking. For all intents and purposes, Chad Royston was just running a personal training program out of his garage. "You put him in the last report. Harrison went to see him the other day."

"That's right. Nobody was home this time, but Harrison went around the back. I parked just down the road while Brian went in to take a look. He wrecked the joint."

A swirl of pure fury erupted in Jesse's chest. "Where is he headed now?"

"We followed him along the road that follows the water. Now he's just parked by the side of the road. I don't know what he's up to, but it's not far from the Moore place."

Jesse closed his eyes as his fingers clenched on his pen. "Watch him like a hawk. And if he looks like he's going to go and start trashing the place, or threaten the Moores, or do anything like that, grab him." He thought about it for a moment, massaging his forehead. Could this get any worse? Why couldn't he have a son like most of the others in the old boy network, kids who were happy to go into the family business, go to uni, get a degree?

"Ignore what he's done at Royston's place," he went on. "If he's into what we think he is, he's not going to be calling the cops. But the Moores' kayaking business—that's different. That'll bring trouble down on us for sure. Just watch him."

"And if he starts something, what do you want us to do with him? Bring him to your house?"

Jesse's mind was in such turmoil he couldn't think of what to do. "Yes. No. Just grab him, sit on him, and then call me. I'll meet you somewhere and take him with me. Alright?"

"Done."

He rang off, and Jesse slumped for a moment at his desk, almost feeling defeated. Just when he had the deal of a lifetime coming through, Harrison was threatening to ruin everything.

Unable to sit still, he stood up and plucked his car keys from the hook on the wall. He'd go down to Sussex himself, ready to intervene.

If this kid ruined everything for him now…

21

A Flash of Silver

LATE IN THE AFTERNOON, Georgie was sitting and staring into her crystal ball, thinking about how she would tackle the fortune-telling tent at the markets, when she felt a niggle of unease.

Within seconds, it had grown into a deep sense of urgency: *Something's wrong.* She reached over to run her fingers across the surface of the smooth globe, frowning, her mind questing.

Scott, sitting across from her and skimming through a travel magazine, pushed his foot against hers under the table. "What's up?"

Georgie's gaze flew up to meet his. "It's that obvious, is it?"

"It is to me." He regarded her curiously and closed the magazine. His eyes moved from hers to the crystal ball, watching her fingers trace a pattern on the surface. "You getting something?"

"There's something…." Georgie shook her head. "I wasn't even thinking about anything. I mean, I was, but it was only about the markets on Saturday and what I might do. Whether to limit the sessions to 15 minutes or let them take as long as they take, within reason. I haven't done public readings for so long."

"It'll probably be a bit of fun for you." Scott studied her for a moment and then reached across and put his hand over hers on the crystal ball. "Do you need to go anywhere? See someone…?"

"Just let me think for a moment." She closed her eyes and let her mind drift. Then, as clear as day, she saw an image of Allie and Chris in her mind.

She opened her eyes again. "It's the Moores. We need to see them, now."

Scott looked at her. "Are you worried about Chris? What he might do?"

"I don't think it's that." Suddenly deciding, she stood up, draped Great-Grandma Rosa's velvet cloth over the crystal ball, and nodded at him. "I just feel as though I need to be there. Coming?"

Scott stood too and gestured at the door. "It's something to fill in the afternoon."

Allie was surprised to see them. She looked from Georgie to Scott, the expression on her face ranging from curious to fearful, followed by a thread of hope. "What is it? Have you found out something?"

Georgie gave her a quick hug. "There's nothing wrong, Allie. I just felt as though I needed to come here. Does that sound crazy?"

Allie gave a wry smile. "No crazier than some of the other stuff you've told me about what you do. But it's lovely to see you, anyway. Come on in." She led the way to the kitchen, throwing over her shoulder as she went, "Emma is so excited about the baby. She did the test today, and it's confirmed!" Reaching the kitchen, she waved at the little table in the sunroom area. "Sit down; I'll get you something to drink. Tea? Coffee?"

"Coffee for me," said Georgie, "but I think Scott will have tea."

Scott nodded. "Yes, tea for me, thanks."

"I'll make a cuppa for Chris, too," Allie said. Her eyes met Georgie's, and she grinned with delight. "I just can't stop thinking about what you said. A lively little girl. With red hair! I can't wait."

Chris came into the kitchen in time to hear her last words. He nodded at Georgie and Scott. "She hasn't stopped talking about anything else since you were here the other night. She and Emma are all about shopping for baby clothes, deciding on names, *un*-deciding on names…."

"Oh, you!" Allie grinned at him. "You're just as excited as I am."

"I guess I am, at that." Chris looked at Georgie. "Are you here for a reason?"

"You're hoping I might have some news for you." Georgie smiled at him sympathetically. "Sorry, Chris, I don't have anything yet." Despite herself, she couldn't help emphasizing the word "yet", and Chris's eyes narrowed a little.

"Yet?" he asked.

"Oh well, you know," Georgie said, grinning at him. "With my direct line to the universe and the knowledge of all that is, something is bound to come to me sooner or later."

"Spoken like a true detective," Scott said lightly. "So, it's 'Grandpa', hey?"

"Grandpa." Chris nodded with a small smile. "Guess he'll be kayaking before he can walk."

"Before *she* can walk," Georgie and Allie said at the same time, which made them both laugh.

"The committee is so excited about your fortune-telling tent, Georgie," Allie said. "The ad ran on local TV last night—did you see it? That stuff about Jesse Burns wife's pendant!" she shook her head. "Fascinating. Do you really think she lost it in a friend's garage?"

"Not quite. I have an idea about where it might have ended up," Georgie said. "But I decided not to say anything to Jesse yet. I, um, want to do a bit more investigating first."

"See?" Scott said, shrugging as he reached for a biscuit. "Psychic detective at work. She follows up her crystal ball hunches with a bit of solid investigation. They'll be making a TV show about her next."

Just as Georgie was about to say something else, they heard the faint sound of voices somewhere outside and a sharp cut-off cry. They all looked at each other, and Allie quickly got up and moved to the window, closely followed by Chris. Outside, the shadows were beginning to lengthen, but looking past her, Georgie could see movement at the edge of the property, near where Chris kept their boat on its trailer.

Chris let out a curse. "*Now* what?" he said, his voice rising at the end of the sentence. "Haven't we had enough?" He hurried to the front door, with the others going after him.

Just past the bushes at the edge of the property, which shielded it from the road, they heard the slam of car doors and then the sound of first one car, then another, speeding away.

"What the hell?" Chris said. He broke into a run, going down to where his boat rested on the gentle grass slope.

"Please, don't let them have done anything to the boat," Allie gasped as she and Georgie followed. Scott had already caught up to Chris, and they both stopped in front of the boat.

Scott immediately reached out to clasp the other man's shoulder. "It's okay, Chris," Scott said, his voice level and reassuring. "It didn't have time to take."

Allie and Georgie reached them and stared at the evidence of flames, hastily put out, with a partly burned cover and some bubbling paint on the coping.

"They tried to set fire to the boat," Chris said, his voice so tired and hopeless that Georgie's heart ached for him.

"Oh, Chris." Allie moved up beside him and put both arms around him. He turned to her and hung onto her as though a drowning man might hold onto a life preserver.

"It's just too much, Allie," he said, his voice low and hopeless. "It's too much. I can't keep fighting this anymore."

"We'll have to call the police," she said, furious. "This vandalism—it has to stop."

Georgie walked over and touched the boat cover, black on the edges. "Chris, I —" She swallowed hard and said, "You've had kayaks vandalized and other stuff disappearing? Right?"

"Yes." He gave one listless inclination of his head.

"And do you think it's just local kids, being vicious and nasty, or you think it's more?"

"I don't know. I just don't know anymore."

Allie tugged him away from the boat. "Come on, Chris. Back to the house. We'll ring the cops, and you can have a drink. I'm going to call Drew and Emma. We all need to have a council of war about this."

"Not tonight," he said dully. "Leave them alone. Maybe tomorrow."

He let her lead him away while Georgie and Scott looked at each other.

"Two cars?" Scott said.

"And there was that yelling, as though—" Georgie's brow creased in a frown as she tried to puzzle it out. "As though there was a disagreement, maybe?" She thought about it for another minute or so. "When we get back, I'll do a reading. I feel this is all coming together, Scott. And the police—they might be able to find something." She looked around. "Maybe footprints, tire tracks —*something*."

As she spoke, the rays of the dying sun slanted down, and something glinted in the grass in front of the boat—a coin. Georgie bent down to check.

No, not a coin. It was a flat metal disc, about the size of a five-cent coin. She picked it up, and held it out on her palm, showing it to Scott. "What do you suppose this—"

Then, with a rush of recognition, she was thrown back to the first reading with Allie and Chris. The image of Harrison in the crystal ball and the glint at his ear. The stretched ear lobes, the metal discs...

She knew with complete certainty that what she was

holding was the disc that Harrison habitually wore in his ear.

In her hand, it grew warm as though confirming her suspicions, and she closed her fingers over it.

Harrison Burns had been here not five minutes before.

Georgie looked at Scott. "Harrison." She opened her palm again and showed him. "This disc, it's out of Harrison's ear—you know how he stretches the lobes? What do they call it?"

Scott nodded. "I don't know what they call it, but I've seen it." His eyes met hers. "What are you going to do? Are you going to give this to the police? Tell Allie and Chris?"

Georgie's mind worked swiftly. She thought about what Bluey had shared with her about Jesse Burns, and she thought about the upcoming fortune-telling stall on Saturday.

Slowly, her lips curved in a smile. For her, it was a very grim smile.

"No," she said. "They don't need it for an insurance claim, and I have a better idea."

Unexpected Visitors

GEORGIE AND SCOTT had been back at the caravan park for only a few minutes when Georgie received a phone call from Emma.

Her first thought was that Drew and Emma had heard about the attempted arson, but as Emma went on, she realized they probably didn't know about it yet.

"Georgie? It's Emma. I was wondering… I know you're going to do readings at the markets on Saturday, but I'd love it if you could find time to fit in one for me and Drew before then?" She hesitated for a moment and then added, "Only if you're not too busy, of course. I know you're here to have a holiday."

Scott was sitting close enough to hear what was being said, and he cast his eyes upward for a minute, a wry smile making his lips curve. Georgie grinned back at him and wrinkled her nose. By now, Scott knew that any vacation with her was probably destined to become a working holiday.

"That's fine, Emma. Of course, you and Drew can have reading."

"I wonder… I mean, would it be too intrusive to come over tonight? Tomorrow, I have this lunch lined up with some of my friends, and Drew has some jobs he has to do, and—"

"Tonight will be fine," Georgie said, choking back a laugh as Scott pretended to bang his head on the table. "And congratulations. Allie tells me that it's a definite yes, now, right?"

"That's right." A note of awe entered Emma's voice. "I still can't get over how you can know that stuff."

"Nothing I like better than delivering good news," Georgie told her. "It's easy to see how much Allie and Chris are looking forward to this. And I'm sure Drew is over the moon, too."

"Yes, he is." Emma's voice was still upbeat, but Georgie thought she heard a note of reserve. *Hmmm.* Was this reading just for fun, or did Emma have another purpose? Remembering her sense that Drew knew more than he was letting on, she was willing to bet on the latter.

"What time would suit?" Emma asked. "We'll come to you, of course. We don't expect you to drive down to us."

Especially since we've just come back from there, Georgie thought. She said: "How about if Scott and I grab an early dinner, and you and Drew come over at about seven? Would that suit?"

"Sounds great. Okay, we'll see you then. What site are you on?"

Georgie told her and then put the phone thoughtfully on the table between her and Scott.

"I can see the wheels turning," he said. "Given what

happened this afternoon, you think there's more to this, don't you?"

Georgie nodded slowly. "But I don't think she's heard anything from Allie and Chris yet. They're probably trying not to rain on her parade."

Scott pushed himself up from the table and went to open the fridge, staring at the contents. "I was thinking a couple of nice scotch fillets tonight, with a fresh salad and a couple of potatoes with sour cream and chives… sound okay to you?"

"Your cooking always sounds good to me." Her mind still on the upcoming reading with Emma, Georgie got up to make the salad. "Let's get this out of the way so we can set up ready for our visitors."

Emma was her usual bubbly self, but coming in behind her, Drew was a man with something on his mind.

Emma looked around her at the interior of the caravan, her eyes sparkling. "Hey, this is great! There's so much room in here. And a place for everything."

"We love it," Georgie admitted. "We don't *have* to stay in a tourist park like this if we don't want to. Free camping your way around Australia is almost akin to staying in a five-star resort these days. We can live off the grid for a couple of weeks; as long as we're near a source of fresh water, we're fine." She indicated the comfortable club seating at the end of the van. "Take a seat, you two."

"I might leave you to it," Scott said. He and Georgie had agreed that Drew might be more ready to open up if it was just Allie and his wife. "Hope you don't mind, guys, but I've got a few calls to make."

"We don't want to intrude." Emma looked at Georgie. "I was thinking; I did kind of dump this on you. Sorry."

"Don't be silly; it's fine." Georgie smiled at her brightly. "Scott often sits outside to do a bit of stuff while I get on with things in here."

Within minutes, they were comfortably settled in the U-shaped seating, with Drew and Emma sitting opposite Georgie.

To ease the two of them into it and make them feel more comfortable, she said to Emma, "I'm surprised that Allie hasn't already been on your doorstep with a bag of baby things. She's so excited about it."

"I know. It's so great, isn't it?" Emma glanced at Drew beside her and gave him a somewhat uncertain smile. "Um, what we wanted to see you about tonight, Georgie—it's kind of related to the baby." She shook her head and started again. "Well, not really. But the baby is part of whatever we do in the future because it's all about family. We have an idea, but we want to know what you think."

Georgie gave a light laugh. "Emma, I don't really do that. Give advice, I mean. I can pass what I see or hear on to you, but it's up to you to make sense of it all and apply it to your life."

Emma nodded vigorously. "I know. I'm not explaining myself very well. Maybe I should let Drew take over." She gave Drew a nudge and nodded at him encouragingly.

When Drew looked at Georgie, she could see indecision mixed with sadness in his eyes. And there was something else, too: the shadow of secrets. She had a sense that it was all becoming too much for him.

"I'm thinking of a change in direction," he said. He cleared his throat and then went on. "All this stuff with dad—I'm worried about him, about Ma. I was thinking if there was a way that we could help turn things around for them, something that would work for us as well, then we should do it."

Georgie nodded and reached out to draw the crystal ball closer to her. Across the table, Emma and Drew's eyes were drawn to the motion, watching the crystal ball intently.

Deep down, Georgie felt the thrill of fulfillment. She would never get tired of this. Briefly, she blessed Great-Grandma Rosa's insistence on making sure she had the crystal ball with her on her very first trip, over a year before. How different her life would have been if she had not experienced this.

Emma spoke up again. "Should we tell you what we are thinking of doing and then see if you have anything to tell us? Or should we just wait?"

With half of her attention still open to the special world that opened up whatever she touched the crystal ball, Georgie raised her eyes and looked at them both. "Well, I hope we have established by now that I'm not a charlatan out to make a few bucks at a psychic fair." Then, anticipating Emma's reaction, she grinned at her. "And that doesn't mean that you should pay for this, by the way. Scott and I are just seeing the sights, and if I can help a few people along the way, that's a bonus."

In response, Emma turned and looked at Drew. "Then tell her, Drew."

He nodded. "You know I've got this business,

where I repair boats, right? I'm a shipwright, so I can build boats too and fit them out. I never wanted to take over dad's business; it wasn't me. But now I'm thinking, if I join forces with him, then he could keep going with all the stuff he loves to do, and I can specialize in doing tours around the basin, plus advise people on taking care of their boats — kind of combine the business I have with something that would help dad."

Emma couldn't help herself; she had to jump in. "But it's not just to help out Allie and Chris. That's a big part of it, of course. Drew wants to help them get back on track, and it's killing us seeing his dad wanting to give up. But we can see the potential in this. We'd just like another perspective on it." Anticipating Georgie's reaction, she held up a hand. "Not giving advice. Just see whether you can see anything through the crystal ball."

Georgie nodded. Under her fingers, the crystal ball was becoming cloudy. She didn't know a lot about Chris's business and how it operated or how Drew might fit in what he wanted to do, but she knew that there was more behind this than he was saying.

"Okay. Well, as I said, I have no idea whether that's a good idea or not, but I will share with you what I find out." She looked up with a laugh. "I do recommend that you consult an accountant or our business advisor as well as a random gypsy psychic."

Emma and Drew both laughed, and the comments served to lighten the atmosphere a bit.

The crystal ball under her fingertips suddenly grew a lot warmer. When she looked down, the mist gradually dissipated, and instead, there was an image of Emma and Drew. Across the table, Emma leaned forward and then gasped when she saw what was there. "Georgie. Is that –?"

Feeling the same glow of pleasure that Emma did, Georgie nodded, her lips parting in a grin. "Yes, that's you and Drew. And, it seems, a new addition to the family."

In the crystal ball, Emma and Drew were standing at the edge of an expanse of water, and there was a new, larger boat moored nearby. Emma was holding a little girl on her hip, a child of about six months of age, her head covered in soft red curls.

Drew, too, had leaned closer to stare. He let out a disbelieving laugh and then turned to look at Emma with an awed smile. "This is crazy. If I hadn't seen it myself, I wouldn't believe it." He shook his head and said to Georgie: "I know you said you don't know how this works, but… I haven't seen anything like this on TV. You know, when they do programs with psychics. Everything you hear is—I don't know, kind of vague."

Pleased by his reaction, Georgie raised her eyebrows at him. "Don't you worry, a lot of what I do is vague at times. But sometimes, it's crystal clear, like now. And I've found that usually, what is in the crystal ball won't show up on film. That's why you'd never see this on TV."

Then abruptly, the image was gone, and instead, there was an image of Drew, standing in front of a door. He reached out to open it and then snatched his hand back again. Again he reached for the door but turned around, and the indecisiveness on his face was clear to all three of them.

"Drew? That's just you." Emma looked at Georgie. "Where is that door? What does that mean?"

Georgie was certain about what it meant, but she

could hardly come out and say that Drew was keeping secrets.

Instead, she forced a look of puzzlement onto her face. "Well,…since the first image of the two of you with the baby in the boat was followed by this, I'm guessing that it means the future you're talking about is possible. It may even show that it's going to happen. But that door—" she looked across to Drew. "I have a sense that there is a door you don't want to go through. Something is holding you back, or…." She shrugged. "Maybe this is just saying that once you open that door and go through it, you've made a decision. Or it could be saying there's a door you don't want to open."

She shrugged. "See what I mean? I can get very clear images, like one of you and Emma and the boat and the baby—and then I can get something like this, that appears to make no sense." She paused and looked at Drew directly. "Unless you take the two together. Sometimes, it's only the person I'm doing the reading for that knows what it all means." She sat back, glancing at the crystal ball, and had to laugh. Drew and the door had been replaced by a row of dominoes, toppling over one by one. Sometimes she thought the universe just liked to laugh at her expense.

"Dominoes?" Emma stared even harder at the ball, her forehead creasing. "Am I seeing *dominoes*?"

"I think you are. And we all know what that means. Once you push over the first domino, then you can't stop the progression. Chain reaction: they all keep tumbling over."

The dominoes disappeared, and in their place, another face formed. Georgie had to control herself not to react when she saw Chad Royston's face in the crystal ball.

When she glanced back at Drew, the color was draining out of his face.

"Drew?" Georgie said sharply. She reached out a hand to touch his. "Drew? Are you okay?"

Across the table, Drew raised his hands to his face, rested his elbows on the table, and hid his face in his hands.

Emma looked at him in alarm. "Drew! What is it?"

"I can't do this anymore," he said. "I have to see Dad. I have to tell him."

The Hacker

When Georgie got through to Bluey, she put the phone on loudspeaker so Scott could hear too.

"Harrison's in *rehab*?" Georgie's eyes widened. "That's a surprise."

"Not when you see the series of messages that I have managed to intercept," Blue told her. "It looks like Jesse Burns has been in damage control for quite some time."

Georgie nodded. "Since the kayaking expedition."

Blue laughed. "I think if you went digging, you'd find that it's been a while longer than that. Harrison's been in trouble for years, dating back to an incident in primary school. He's on a downhill slope, and I don't think there's a lot that Jesse can do to stop it."

"Even with all his money and connections?" Scott put in.

"He's got a long reach, that's for sure. But money can't buy everything."

Scott looked across the Georgie. "Have you got enough now to pull off what you're planning?"

"Yes, I think so." Just checking, Georgie ticked off a

list on her fingers. "Bluey, you don't want me to mention anything about Angelo McKay, right?"

"Absolutely not. That's a subject of an ongoing investigation, and the Feds are getting close to an arrest. Jesse is going to get caught up in it all, so don't tip him off." His voice changed a little. "Georgie, be careful. This guy's got connections you wouldn't want to know about."

"I hear you. But do you think that I could persuade him to do what I ask so that all this doesn't get out?"

Bluey snorted. "With the deal that he's just pulled off? The guy's loaded. Just be careful how you phrase it, and I think you'll be okay."

Georgie bit her lip. "This investigation you're talking about, Bluey… that's not likely to go down before I can persuade him to do everything that we talked about?"

"You should be fine. I'd say we're about a month, maybe six weeks out. When I say "close", I'm talking in a context of an investigation that has been going on for eighteen months."

"Thanks, Bluey." Georgie underlined a few of the words she had written down, including the name of the facility where Harrison had been taken. "Anything else I should know?"

This time Scott answered. "Tell her anything else, and you'd have to kill her, right, Bluey?"

"You're not far wrong. Just stick to the call he got from Meteor Bronze Holdings, the facility where Harrison is being held, and mention the two shell companies I told you about. That's enough to get him rattled, and it leaves the bigger stuff for us."

Georgie sent back with a sense of satisfaction. "Thanks. It looks like we've got him. People like him, well—" she shrugged. "I know Rosa would probably say that I should let the universe take care of it all, that he will get what he deserves, but the problem is Chris Moore might go down first and sink without a trace. I can't let that happen." She thought of Emma, Drew, and the laughing redheaded baby, and gave a decisive nod. This time, she would see to it that the little guys had a bit of help.

"Anyway, guys, I have to go. You owe me. So when are you going to come across and see me in WA?"

Scott leaned forward to address the phone. "Well, see, we're not sure that you do *live* in WA. We think you're a spook."

"You just keep on thinking that. See you later, guys."

Georgie put down the phone and looked up at Scott's slow chuckle. "What?"

"I'm quite sure that Rosa didn't deal in so much intrigue," he said. "Now, *there* was a real old-fashioned gypsy fortune teller. You, on the other hand...." He shook his head, his eyes sparkling with laughter. "You're turning into quite the vigilante, aren't you?"

"It's not as though I'm taking out anyone's kneecaps or anything," Georgie said primly. "I'm just... planting seeds, that's all. And Jesse Burns, well, I guess he's finally reaping what he sowed, right?"

"Right." Then his face became sober. "Do you think Drew is going to tell Chris what he told us?"

"No, I don't think so. Not yet, anyway. He knows that Chris is too fragile to hear something like that at the moment. Later, I think he probably will. But it wouldn't achieve anything now, would it?"

"For someone who told him you were not going to give advice," said Scott, "you had a thing or two to say."

Georgie shrugged and got up to make coffee. "He came to see whether he should go into business with his father. I left that up to him—and I'm still leaving it up to him. All I can do is tell him what I saw; that things look promising."

"But you told him to hold off telling his father about Royston until you've had a chance to put some pressure on Jesse."

"That, too." Georgie ruffled his hair. "Okay, I'm an interfering gypsy. So sue me."

"Don't need to," Scott said confidently, getting up to get the milk out of the fridge. "The universe will always step in. I've seen it happen often enough."

"True," Georgie said. "But this time, it's getting some help from me."

"And Bluey."

She grinned. "And Bluey."

24

An Understanding

Jesse Burns felt worn out.

If it hadn't been for the Meteor Bronze Holdings development coming through, it would have been one of the worst weeks he'd had.

Sitting back in the lounge room with his wife and daughter, he sipped slowly on his Glenmorangie whiskey, replaying recent events in his mind.

Harrison stealing jewelry, taking off in his mother's car, then seeing a known or suspected drug dealer at the pub, followed by vandalism at Chad Royston's place and then a touch of arson at Chris Moore's. It was unbelievable. How could he have given birth to such a child?

His only consolation was that Harrison was, at long last, safely locked away. In a rehab facility, that was, thank God, more like a prison for people with money. At least he was out of harm's way for the time being. It would give all of them time to regroup.

His wife tossed back a mouthful of wine and said again, "So you couldn't get out of him what he's done with the butterfly pendant?"

Jesse mentally counted to three, and with a huge effort, kept his voice level when he replied. "I may be able to persuade him to tell me in time, Jenna, but at the moment, I've got other things to worry about. Just be grateful that the little so-and-so isn't under our roof anymore."

Jenna grimaced. "Where did we go wrong? Nicholas and Leah, they're both fine—well, Leah tends to party too much and get home too late, but she is going to be okay, you can tell. Nicholas, we can be proud of him. But Harrison?" She put her glass of wine on the coffee table in front of her and sat forward, resting her forehead on her hand while she stared at the carpet. "I wish he was still overseas. I wish he would just go away, and *stay* away, and leave us alone." She closed her eyes for a beat and then looked up at him. "Can you organize that?"

"I've been considering how I can achieve exactly that," Jesse said, drinking more of the whiskey. "It's not going to work to give him a job in anything I'm involved with. We can't trust him, and he has no inclination to work for what he wants. I'm thinking probably overseas if I can manage it."

Jenna abruptly stood up. "Bribe him, if you have to, so he'll tell me where that pendant went. I don't care if we have to pay twice as much as it's worth to get it back, but I want it."

Jesse nodded slowly. "All right, Jenna. All in good time. For now, I've got to get these stupid seasonal markets over and done with and then sign off on a few other deals that will make a huge difference to our financial future. I can buy you a dozen butterfly pendants and not even notice."

"Well, that's very nice, Jesse, but you know that's not the point." Jenna stood up, turned on her heel, and left the room. "I'm going to bed."

As she left the room, the door chimes sounded. He heard Leah going to the door and answering, and then she appeared in the doorway. "Dad? There's someone here to see you."

He looked at her wearily. "Who the hell is it?"

"No idea. Some slimy loser. I'm going upstairs."

With a groan, Jesse got up and went to the door. He recognized the person standing on the mat, and his brows immediately drew together in a frown. "What do *you* want?"

Chad Royston held up his phone. "I have a video on my phone that you need to see. And a lot of damaged equipment that needs to be paid for."

Bluffing it out, Jesse just raised an eyebrow and folded his arms. "And would you mind telling me what this has to do with me?"

"It has a lot to do with you," said Chad. His gaze bored into Jesse's eyes. "You see, I've installed security cameras around my home gym because it has a lot of valuable equipment in it. I've also installed cameras in the house. Your son wasn't able to break in the house—let's be thankful for small mercies—but I've got some excellent footage of him trashing my place."

Plenty of thoughts went through Jesse's mind. Uppermost was: *Will this never end?* Closely followed by: *Thanks, Harrison, that's all I need, trash like this on my doorstep.* He looked at the phone, still held up by Chad, and hesitated for a moment. His instincts were to tell the kid to get lost, but clearly, he wasn't prepared to go through the police. He was here because he knew the damage that the video footage would do to Jesse Burns' reputation.

"Your choice," Chad said. "We can come to an arrangement to pay for the damage, or I go to the police, and this goes viral."

"Why is it," Jesse said coldly, "that I feel you are most unlikely to go to the police?"

"Possibly," Chad said in an equally unfriendly tone, "because we understand each other. Don't worry; this is not about blackmail. It's just about making good the damage."

Somehow, Jesse felt deep in his heart that with people like Chad Royston, it was never just about adequate compensation for whatever wrongs had been done. No, that footage on Chad Royston's phone would stay there and probably rest on a thumb drive somewhere until the next time he wanted to exert pressure.

Well, he knew people too. And if Chad chose to take it further, he'd regret it.

"Come in," he said and stood back to let his enemy through the door.

25

Market Day

"THEY COULDN'T HAVE HAD A BETTER day for this," Georgie said, strolling through the expansive waterfront markets with her fingers interlinked with Scott's. She turned her face up to the sun. "What glorious weather."

"They were pretty lucky. At this time of year, you can never be sure what you're going to get." Scott tugged her in the direction of one of the food stalls. "Are we ready to have breakfast yet? I'm starving."

"Sure." Georgie looked at her watch. "We've got a while until the fortune-telling tent is due to open." She was glad that she had decided to spend some time wandering around before she opened up. This was just too lovely to miss.

Scott wandered over to where a school parents' group was busy turning out dozens of egg and bacon rolls, sausage sandwiches, or tubs of fruit salad for those who prefer to eat light. "Want an egg and bacon roll?"

"Not for me, thanks. I'll take the fruit salad. By lunchtime, I'll be ready for something a bit more substantial."

Georgie stood back and waited while Scott went to fetch breakfast, taking in the variety of stalls and tents and gazebos lined up along the waterfront. Jewelry stalls, food outlets, lapidary and rocks, general trash and treasure, plenty of potted plants and seedlings, and at least half a dozen tents decked out with racks of clothes. Down towards the end, she knew there was a stall from the local scuba diving center, advertising their courses, and a jumping castle and pony rides for the kids.

In one corner, she could see a gazebo with racks full of BoHo clothes that would be perfect for her. She gravitated towards that kind of outfit anyway, nice and light and comfortable, plus that sort of stuff meant that she always had a wardrobe of clothes for her Gypsy persona if she wanted it. She'd go down and investigate later, she decided.

Scott returned with his egg and bacon roll and handed her the fruit salad. Then his eyes fixed on something over her shoulder. "Action stations. The camera crew is here, following Jesse Burns around."

Georgie didn't turn around. "Is he coming this way?"

"Nope. Too busy being Mr. Big, nodding and smiling at all the also-rans, slapping people on the back… don't know why the guy isn't a politician."

"It could happen," she said. "He wouldn't be the first businessman who decided he wants to wield more power and influence."

"And to get on the gravy train forever."

Georgie nodded towards a group of tables and chairs, where a dozen other people were enjoying breakfast while they gazed around them. Not far away, a trio was setting up with microphones and amplifiers, and she could hear a guitar twanging. Georgie dipped into her fruit salad. Delicious: full-bodied, sweet, juicy. "Yum."

"Now he's being filmed over there at the *A Taste of the Coast* stall," Scott informed her before taking a huge bite of his breakfast roll. He kept up the running commentary while he ate. "Yup, doing a taste test, having a few words to the proprietor. And… now he's making a beeline for the farmer's market produce."

"As long as he stays away long enough for me to enjoy my breakfast." Feeling a little queasy at the thought of having to deal with him later, Georgie directed her attention to the musical trio. She noticed the blackboard beside them, with the names of five or six different performers. "This is well organized. I mean, we've been to a zillion markets, but this is one of the better ones."

"Georgie!" A voice sang out from not far away, and this time Georgie turned around, recognizing Allie's voice.

"Hi, Allie. Sit down. Isn't this great? It's going to be so good for the area. How's Chris this morning?"

"He's not too bad. It's almost as though so much bad stuff has happened that he's becoming desensitized." She sighed. "Which is not great. I think it's doing him good to be here; talk to some of his friends." Allie looked around her and gave a nod of satisfaction. "This *does* look good. It was a lot of work, setting it all up, rounding people up to participate, getting the business people involved—but the closer it got, the more involved they all got, too. I think it'll all be worth it."

"You should be proud of yourself, Allie," Georgie said. "It's people like you that towns need. Those who don't just sit by and let others do it, but take action."

Allie went faintly pink with pleasure. "Thank you, Georgie. It's nice of you to say so." She opened her mouth to say something else, but Georgie forestalled her, holding up a hand. "And don't tell me that it takes a committee and that a whole lot of other people helped too; I know all that." She grinned at Allie. "Just take the kudos."

"Okay then. I will." Allie looked around her and then leaned over to say conspiratorially, "I just thought I'd duck over to see you while Chris is busy talking to a couple of his cronies over at the local business owners' table. I'm really nervous. Do you honestly think you can make Jesse Burns fix things?"

Allie just smiled at her and gave one slow, definite nod, then sampled another spoonful of fruit salad before she spoke again. "I'm pretty sure of it. Of course, you can never tell with someone like Jesse Burns; they always think that they're so privileged and untouchable. But…" She shrugged. "Armed with the crystal ball, plus a bit of knowledge from sources I can't divulge, I think we're going to see him pretty rattled, at least. And even if he doesn't agree to anything today, I think once he goes home to think about it, you might see something."

Allie nodded and then pulled a face. "This is torture. Can't you give me just a little clue?"

"No, she can't," Scott said breezily, treating Allie to one of his full-wattage smiles. "Highly confidential sources. If Georgie tells you, they may have to kill her."

For a moment, Allie's face fell, and Scott added quickly, "Just kidding. But we do know things, Allie, that we can't tell you about. What Georgie sees in the crystal ball is true enough, but…." He shot a sideways look at Georgie. "Let's just say that we know people. Jesse Burns is not the only one who has contacts." He finished off the last few mouthfuls of his roll and crumpled up the paper it had been wrapped in. "And now, Georgie, I think you've been sprung. Showtime! Here comes the film crew."

Georgie was glad that they'd had plenty of time to walk around first. She snapped the top back on the container of half-eaten fruit salad and handed it to Scott to put in his backpack. Then she shouldered her capacious bag (there was no way she was going to leave Great-Grandma Rosa's crystal ball unattended in a tent on oceanfront markets) and stood up, the weight of the crystal ball bumping comfortably against her side.

"I'd better get back to Chris. Good luck." Allie's eyes met Georgie's, and in her gaze, Georgie saw a silent plea. "I'll catch up with you later."

Allie turned and walked away, saying in a cheerful voice as she passed Jesse Burns, "Good morning, Jesse. A wonderful day for our inaugural markets, isn't it?" Then she kept sailing past, not waiting for his response. However, one of the camera crew called after her, "Allie! Hang on. Have you got a minute?"

Allie paused in her flight and turned around to look at him. Even at a distance, Georgie could hear what he said. "A few people have mentioned your name; one of them pointed you out a minute ago. Said you're one of the prime forces behind all this. Can we grab a couple of minutes of your time, just do a quick sound bite?"

Allie looked flustered. "I'm not really a publicity-type person."

"It'll only take up about ten seconds on the final piece," the cameraman reassured her. "Maybe over there against the background of the inlet? The water is so beautiful today, and we can film the tents in a row behind you…just for a second?"

Allie looked back at Georgie, and Georgie gave a nod and a thumbs up. Allie should get some of the credit for all her work.

Allie capitulated. "Okay then, I guess that would be all right. Just a few minutes?"

"Just a few minutes," the cameraman promised. He glanced back to where Jesse was just walking up to Georgie. "Georgie, are you right to do a piece with Jesse in front of your tent after that?"

Georgie looked at Jesse and smiled at him, a cheerful smile that said it was a beautiful day and she had nothing she wanted to do more than to walk around the markets and enjoy what he had put together.

"Sure," she said. "Jesse can be my very first customer. I'm looking forward to it."

By now, he had reached her. His smile remained fixed, but his eyes didn't carry any amusement at all, as he said, "Me too. Nothing I like better than having my fortune told."

"I think you'll be surprised," Georgie said, "at the amazing things your future will hold."

———————

26

Reeling in the Fish

———————

ALLIE HAD EXCELLED herself in setting up the fortune-teller's tent. Knowing that Georgie wanted a private space to do her readings—and, more importantly, to have a private conversation with Jesse Burns—she had planned it carefully. The "tent" was a gazebo, but Allie had scavenged deep scarlet silk from somewhere to create walls. She had erected a kind of porch at the front and placed on it a table draped in black, where Scott was going to engage with people who were waiting for Georgie. He had drawn the line, however, at dressing up in anything that remotely resembled Gypsies.

"I'll just take my seat here," he said to Georgie, dropping a quick kiss on her temple. "You go inside and do your thing."

The camera crew got busy drawing back one wall to let in some light without sacrificing any of the feeling of warmth and mystery that Allie had managed to create. She'd found a round table somewhere and placed two deckchairs, draped with embroidered scarves, on either side of it.

On another smaller table in a corner rested a flickering LED candle. The shimmering light reflected off the glowing surface of the crystal ball, which Georgie placed in the center of the main table.

Satisfied, Georgie nodded. It was the perfect place to talk to people, to give them value, as well as a bit of fun.

"Nice setup," said the cameraman approvingly. He set up his tripod and directed them where to sit, moving the chairs closer together. "We'll get some establishing shots later, showing you walking towards the tent, Jesse. I'll capture Georgie's face as you walk in, and then maybe you can ham it up a bit, look back at the camera, make some comment about wondering what you're going to find out today."

Jesse settled into the chair next to Georgie; the two of them angled slightly towards each other so the camera could capture the expressions on both faces.

"Okay, soundcheck," the assistant said, glancing between Georgie and the cameraman. "You first, Mr. Burns."

Jesse said a few words, and then it was Georgie's turn, and the assistant gave a thumbs up. "If you mess things up, feel free to start again. But don't worry about it too much; just let it flow naturally. The stuff we got on the beach was pure gold, so maybe we can start by following up on that?"

When they nodded, he went on: "Jesse, maybe you can tell Georgie you have news for her after what she predicted on the beach. Or perhaps Georgie could ask how her previous predictions panned out?"

"I'll start," Jesse jumped in. That didn't surprise Georgie — Jesse had always struck her as the type who would want to take the lead. She smiled at him and nodded.

The cameraman counted them in, and Jesse turned slightly towards Georgie. He looked at the crystal ball and then looked back at her, a slow grin growing on his face. "Remember when you did that reading for me on the beach, Georgie? You told me I'd be having good news coming, a business deal?"

"Of course," Georgie said, looking interested and approachable. "So, how did I do?"

"What can I say?" Jesse spread his hands expansively. "You were right. It wasn't quite the news of the century because I've always got so many business deals on my plate at any one time, but yes, I did get news that one of my developments got the green light."

"So it wasn't such a big deal?" She gave a convincing chuckle. "That's how it goes with the crystal ball. It can tap into things; it can show me what's going to happen. But sometimes, the size of the event might not measure up. At least you *did* get news."

"I did. My accountant rang me to let me know that the council had approved a development application for a new shopping center down the coast. Just a strip mall, but it will make a difference to the locals. So, yes, I'm pretty happy about that."

Liar, Georgie thought while still keeping her expression open and appreciative. She knew perfectly well what news Jesse had received, and it wasn't for any small strip mall. The deal was buried a couple of layers deep, through a shell corporation, and he wouldn't want *that* getting out.

"You also mentioned my wife's missing pendant," Jesse

said. "Well, I'm afraid we weren't able to track that down. We did ask around, but nobody has seen it." He grinned. "They all made a point of checking their garages. So I'm afraid that might be gone unless you can give me more specific information today?" He reached over and tapped her folded hands, linked together in front of the crystal ball. It was just a light touch, but it made Georgie's flesh creep.

Which was probably what he intended. Jesse Burns was a man who liked to intimidate.

"That could well happen," she said easily. "When I have successive readings with the same person, often the information I get builds up. Sometimes one of us will get further insights. If that happens, of course, I'll share them with you."

"And cut," said the cameraman. He straightened up pushed back his headphones. "That was a really good start. Maybe we can get a picture of the plans of that strip mall, or the model. Whatever you've got, Jesse. We can flash that up on the screen. And I don't suppose you have a photo of the pendant you were talking about, do you?"

"I do," Jesse said. "We have photographs of every-thing for the insurance company. I'll get it to you later today."

"Let's keep going, then." The cameraman gave them a nod. "Just follow it through, Georgie. Do your thing; we can cut it later." He looked at his assistant. "After we're done here, we'll spend another hour or so wandering around, get Jesse's opening speech, take a few shots of people having fun; then we can take it back and edit."

He settled his headphones in place, bent over slightly

to look at the screen, and then gave a thumbs-up. "And we're rolling."

Georgie pulled the crystal ball towards her. Her mind was on what she intended to say to Jesse Burns after the film crew had gone, but she was also looking forward to seeing what she might pick up with him beside her.

Her wrist was still tingling from where he had touched her. She gave an inward smile. If he had known that touch could make a difference, could help her tap into the person, he no doubt would have thought twice about doing that.

27

Show Time

"Do you have a question in mind, Mr. Burns?" Georgie sent him a non-threatening smile. "Or shall I just see what comes?"

Jesse pretended to consider her words, and then he said, "You're a fortune teller, right? So let's run with that. You can tell me my fortune." He smiled back at her, but there was a definite challenge in his eyes.

Right, thought Georgie. *If that's how we're going to play it.* She nodded and looked down at the crystal ball, smoothing her fingers over it before sitting with her hands cupped around the globe, her eyes closed. Perhaps it was because today was so important, or maybe it was just that the universe thought Jesse Burns might need to get his comeuppance, but things started happening very quickly.

Jesse Burns, fortune. She let her mind drift, encompassing all that those words might mean.

"You said you have a lot of business deals going on," she said, speaking softly and not opening her eyes. "I sense that there are several that are going to be finalized very soon."

"That's right." Jesse's voice sounded faintly mocking. "But as you have pointed out, that's always the case with me. You know what they say: *'if you're not growing, you're dying'.*"

It was time. Georgie moved her hands aside and let them rest on the table at the base of the stand on which the crystal ball stood and looked to see what it had to tell her.

She saw what was in the crystal ball at the same time Jesse did. His eyes narrowed, and then he glanced up at her before focusing on the small figure that that appeared. He was looking at an image of himself, just standing there with his hands held out in front of him, palms up. Then, as if out of nowhere, piles of banknotes appeared, stacked up on his hands like a small mountain. The image in the crystal ball grew smaller and smaller, and the stack of money grew higher and higher. Then, all at once, there was a flurry of wind inside the crystal. Within seconds all the money had been carried away, spiraling away from the small Jesse Burns in the globe.

Then he, too, disappeared, and the crystal ball was empty.

To Georgie, the message was clear, even if she *hadn't* known that Jesse Burns was likely to be stripped of a lot of his assets. Money was flowing away from Jesse Burns, not towards him. You might say money was being ripped out of his hands.

She heard a slight gasp from the cameraman but ignored it and looked Jesse in the eye. "It looks like you're going to have to part with a large amount of money, Jesse. But I guess that's par for the course when you invest in so many business activities, right?" This time, it was her turn to let him see that she wasn't telling the whole story.

He managed to hide the flicker of unease in his eyes and forced a laugh. "That's so right." He met her eyes for a moment, and she knew he was able to interpret what he saw as well as she could. "I would have liked to have seen an image of some of it coming *back* to me, too. But maybe that will happen in the next reading."

"Maybe." Georgie passed her palms over the surface of the crystal ball, willing an image to appear. There must be more than this…

"That missing pendant," Jesse said suddenly. "I don't want to harp on it, but it meant a lot to my wife. Can you try again, see if there is anything else you can tell me about that?"

She glanced at him and thought of the blue house that she'd sensed the last time they'd had a reading. She was almost certain that the pendant was still somewhere on Chad Royston's property, but she hadn't planned to tell Jesse that. It could be useful as a bargaining chip for later.

Then, opposite her, Jesse made a sudden move, leaning forward to stare at the crystal ball, his mouth opening wide. "My God."

Before she looked down, Georgie knew what she was going to see. Sure enough, there was the butterfly pendant, gleaming and winking from the depths of the crystal ball. It appeared to be resting in a nest of tissue paper.

"Do you see that?" she asked Jesse, knowing already that he could but wanting the cameras to catch it. "I'm assuming that what we can see in the crystal ball is your wife's pendant?"

"That's it." Jesse leaned forward, and his fingers clenched on the edge of the table. He tried to keep his voice under control, but she could hear the mix of anger and hope in it. "But where is it?" He looked up at her. "You said if we keep a question in our minds, that that might help to find the answers we want. So that's the question I have: *where is my wife's pendant?*"

Georgie almost ended it there, closing her eyes while she pretended to consider the question—but just as she was about to tell him that it seemed the answer was not going to be revealed today, she heard a soft voice in her mind. *Let the crystal ball decide.*

She relaxed. Fine. Who was she, after all, to control this? She opened her mind to the question in Jesse's mind.

Where is the butterfly pendant?

If the universe wanted Jesse Burns to know, it could show him.

Together, she and Jesse stared into the depths of the crystal. For a moment, the butterfly pendant winked back at them, and then things changed. The perspective altered, as though a camera was drawing back away from the pendant. It became evident that the glittering butterfly was in a box. She could see the glint of other jewelry around it peeking out from the folds of tissue paper.

The imaginary camera drew back further, and for a fraction of a second, they saw a shoebox with the lid half off, revealing the contents. In the blink of an eye, it was gone.

Georgie raised her eyes. In the split second before

the image disappeared, she'd seen a black and white drawing outline of a jogging shoe on the side of the box, along with printed information about sizing. The question was, had Jesse noticed that, too?

"There's your answer," she said. "Well, part of it, anyway. It looks as though the pendant is being kept in a box, but as to where that box is…?" She shrugged.

Jesse looked at her. " Last time, you said you saw it in someone's garage. Now it's in a box. Does that mean that it's being stored in a shoebox in a garage?"

Georgie considered his question. She felt certain that the box was still in Chad Royston's garage, but again, she was reluctant to release that information. "You saw the box?" she asked cautiously.

"I saw it."

"I don't know if the pendant has been moved and put in that box or whether it is still where I first sensed it was," Georgie said. "Find the owner of the shoes that came in that box, and that might help you find out where it is."

Jesse let out a frustrated laugh. "Yeah, right. That's going to be easy; I don't think. How many thousands of people have bought a pair of jogging shoes?"

Thousands, Georgie mentally agreed. But cross trainers, size 10? She wouldn't mind betting that those shoes would be on Chad Royston's feet or in his closet.

"Okay. We'll let that go for now." Jesse no longer looked like the smug man who had strolled into the tent. "Can you see anything else you'd like to tell me today?" Again, he reached over and touched her hand. Georgie hated him doing that; with the type of man Jesse Burns was, it felt like an invasion of privacy. To shake him off, she moved her hands back to touch the crystal ball, rubbing it softly.

Images crashed into her mind, one after another. Harrison curled up on a bed somewhere, tossing restlessly. Jesse's wife Jenna, the woman she had seen on his arm earlier, her face twisted and angry, accusing. And then, flicking from one image to another so quickly she could barely absorb it, she saw a courtroom, a judge, and Jesse sitting there, his shoulders bowed.

She stole a panicked look at the crystal ball and then let out a silent sigh of relief. There was nothing there for him to see. The images were in her mind only.

Jesse was not going to be the man of influence he was now for much longer. By the end of the year, he would be in a very different place.

She looked at him. "I do have one or two pieces of information for you, Jesse—but they are more private. Perhaps I could see you for a few minutes before you open the markets?"

He stared at her and then down at the crystal ball, showing nothing but the swirling white mist.

"What, right now?"

"If you don't mind," Georgie said. "I think that would be best before you get caught up in the rest of the day. I know you've got lots happening. These markets are a real credit to you and the committee." She sent him another sunny smile, which marginally seemed to ease his worried expression.

He managed to smile and then gave a slow hand clap. "Well, I must say that you have managed to change my mind about crystal balls and fortune-tellers. You won't be offended if I tell you that I was not convinced before this... but you have certainly given me something to think about." His eyes fell on the crystal ball again, and again she saw him suppress an expression of unease.

"Thank you, Jesse." She picked up the cloth that she used to cover the crystal ball and gently let it drift down over the top of it. "I hope we can have lots of satisfied people walking away from this stall today."

As one, they turn to the cameraman.

He stopped the recording and gave them an enthusiastic thumbs up. "Great stuff."

Jesse got up and went over to stand behind the tripod, looking at the playback screen. "Can you run it back to where we saw the box that the jewelry is in?"

Georgie watched him, knowing what would happen because she'd been through it before.

Sure enough, when the footage returned to the scene where she and Jesse were talking about the butterfly pendant, the cameraman let out a sound of frustration. "Nothing." He hit a few buttons and then adjusted the zoom. The image of the crystal ball filled the screen, but there was nothing to be seen. To the viewer, it would be just an innocent-looking glass ball.

Georgie had been filmed many times, but the camera had never managed to capture the secrets that lay in the depths of the crystal ball. That was for her and her alone—and sometimes, her customers, although not even all of them were able to see what was in the crystal ball.

She got up and walked across to them. "Sorry, guys. I'm afraid that happens whenever I'm being filmed. I can see what's in the crystal ball, and often my customers can, too, like Jesse did today. But for some reason, it doesn't translate to film."

The cameraman's assistant let out a grunt of frustration. "I can't believe we didn't get it on camera! I *saw* it."

Jesse turned to him eagerly. "You saw it too?"

"Not clearly, because I was over here. But I saw something in there, yes."

Jesse shook his head and then glanced at his watch and the camera crew. "Do you guys mind waiting outside for a minute? It seems like Georgie has more to tell me. I'll be out in a moment."

"Sure thing," said the cameraman. "But first, can we shoot a few noddies? Won't take long."

No newcomer to filming, Georgie knew what he meant. "Come on," she said to Jesse. "They just want to shoot a few of your reactions."

It took only a minute for the camera crew to get close-up shots of her saying things to Jesse, his face looking intent and impressed as he nodded, listening to her, and then they packed up and were out of there. The cameraman looked back at her, regret on his face. She knew he would love to hear what else she had to say. Smiling at him, she disconnected the microphone and handed it over. There was no way he was going to be able to listen in surreptitiously.

He grinned back, shrugged, and walked out.

She nodded at Jesse's microphone. "You might want to turn that off."

Jesse did so and then turned to her, his body tense. "All right, what is it? You saw something that you don't want on camera?"

"Quite a bit, Mr. Burns." Georgie went to the door of the tent and said to Scott, who was sitting at the table outside, "Scott, can you make sure we're not disturbed for a moment?"

Scott winked. "Sure thing."

Georgie reached up and unhooked the opaque curtain that offered complete privacy to whoever was in the tent, let it swish into place, and then turned back to Jesse, bathed in the cozy warm glow afforded by the silky red fabric.

Cozy was absolutely the wrong word for what Jesse was going to be feeling in a moment.

28

More Revelations

Jesse looked at her with an expression that spoke of both suspicion and apprehension. She returned his gaze thoughtfully, and he seemed to understand that he would not like what he was going to hear. "You have more news for me?"

"Yes." Georgie glanced outside and saw the camera crew still there, standing a little too close. She nodded towards the table, which Allie had placed at a confidential distance from the doorway. "Come over here, Jesse."

She sat in one of the deckchairs and leaned back. Jesse's eyes went to the crystal ball, now covered by the worn black velvet cloth that had accompanied it through the years.

"Jesse." Georgie considered how to start, but he took charge again before she could get another word out.

"How reliable is what you see?"

Georgie allowed a small smile to creep onto her face. "I'm not going to defend or justify what I do to you, Jesse. You've seen it for yourself. Do you honestly think that I am using some remote control, some wireless device to create the images you see?" On impulse, she bent forward, tweaked off the black cloth, and carefully picked up the globe from its embellished stand. "Hold out your hands, and cup them."

Slowly, Jesse did what she asked. As the weight of the crystal ball settled into his hands, Georgie took hers away. "Be careful," she said. "That crystal ball has survived many generations, from my grand great-grand-mother's grandmother and probably beyond. It's very precious."

"Ha." He held the ball up and squinted at it, the crimson silk walls lending at a rosy glow. Carefully, he turned it around in his hands, examining it.

"You can see through it, right?" Georgie asked. "You can see that there are no wires, nothing. It is exactly what it appears to be: a crystal ball. I have no control over what appears in it, just as I have no control over whether *you* can see anything or not."

"Well, I did see *something*." He handed her back the crystal ball, and Georgie polished it lightly with the cloth before sitting it back in its stand and covering it again. "And so did the camera crew. But it didn't show up on the video."

"No," said Georgie. "And if I'd somehow been projecting it into the crystal ball, they should have picked it up, right?"

Jesse threw up his hands and sat back in the chair, looking at her challengingly. "All right. Let's assume that this is for real, and you have seen things—"

"Things that you have seen yourself," Georgie pointed out. "I didn't force you to see anything."

Jesse waved that away. "Yet you saw something else —something I didn't see."

Georgie nodded. "That's the way it works. To me, the crystal ball is a medium—it's just a way that I can access whatever knowledge is out there that I can pick up. And it's not just images I see in the crystal ball. Sometimes in my mind, I hear words: sometimes, I see words. At other times I just have…." She shrugged. "It sounds dramatic to say I have a vision or a revelation, but that's what it is. Sometimes I just know."

Deliberately, Jesse looked at his watch. "I do have to keep moving. So if you wouldn't mind…."

Georgie took a deep breath and set up a little straighter in her chair. "Does the name Meteor mean anything to you?"

Opposite her, Jesse froze. His eyes narrowed. "Meteor? You're telling me that you heard this word? Or saw it in your mind?"

"I can see by your face that you do know what I'm talking about," Georgie said. She swallowed, trying not to let Jesse see her nervousness. To her relief, her voice was steady as she went on. "I have some names, too. Martin Carrick. Annabel Pawley. Bruno Schmidt."

Jesse put both hands on the table, his fist clenched. "I don't believe you. You didn't just hear those names. Who sent you?"

Well, there's confirmation that I've struck gold, Georgie thought. "It is true that sometimes I do pick up a name or a nickname—something that needs looking into. And when I saw you last time, I saw names that I felt should be investigated further."

"Investigated further." Jesse bit the words out, his eyes hard. "Who *are* you?" His eyes went to the tank top she wore under the embroidered soft scarf, as though suspecting that she was wearing a wire. "I don't know that we need to continue any further."

He went to stand up, but Georgie held up a hand to stop him. "Please, Jesse. I think you should hear me out."

"And if I choose not to?"

"If you choose not to," Georgie said, "I may have to make it known that the good news you got just after our first reading had nothing to do with the strip mall down the coast. It had *everything* to do with the heritage-listed property that certain people are trying to demolish so that you can build your block of units." She waited for a beat before mentioning the name of the shell company he'd used.

Opposite her, Jesse's face grew pale. For a moment, Georgie thought about the other information that Bluey had passed on. If Jesse realized how much she knew, he'd be catching the first plane out of the country.

Jesse's lips grew tight, and he sat back and folded his arms. "And what do you plan to do with this information?"

Reminding herself that his day would come, Georgie just shook her head at him, smiled gently, and said, "Nothing."

"Nothing." He let out a crack of laughter. "I don't for one minute imagine you would have bothered telling me all this if there wasn't something you wanted from me."

Here it was. She couldn't muck this up: couldn't make things any worse for Chris and Allie. The responsibility weighed heavy.

"You're right," she said. "There is something I want

—but it's not for me. I just need you to undo some of the damage you have done, and then we can call it quits." *Quits,* she thought, *until whatever Bluey is talking about finally closes in on you.*

"Undo some of the damage." He smiled mercilessly. "I don't know what you mean. I make every effort not to damage people. I always pay compensation; I always go through the proper channels." Again, his eyes went to her chest, and Georgie knew that he was worried she was trying to entrap him.

She tapped her chest and shook her head at him. "You do not need to worry that I'm anyone other than who I say I am. But you're not the only one with contacts, and you're not the only one that has people with certain skills at their beck and call." She met his eyes. "I've been called a psychic detective by some. I'm not interested in bringing anyone down; no one employs me. But I do like to see the little guys get a win. Especially against people like you, who have far too much power and influence for their own good."

Jesse narrowed his eyes again and looked as though he was contemplating a walkout. His hands tensed on the table, but Georgie forestalled him with a hand in the air. "Last year," she said, "your son Harrison caused an accident because of the drugs he took at a school kayaking program."

After what she had been saying about his business deals, this was not what he had expected. Taken aback, he scowled. "Unfortunately, that is fairly common knowledge. And Harrison has paid for that. He was expelled from school, and his life effectively ruined."

Georgie shook her head. "No. *Ruined* is what you did to Chris Moore. A man who hasn't done anything wrong, who has always tried to do the right thing by his family, his clients, and the local community." She looked at him steadily, remembering Jesse's words: "*Jesse Burns blames me. So he finishes me off for no good reason other than he needs revenge.*"

Jesse looked impatient. "What happened to Chris Moore had nothing to do with me. White Sands College had a zero-tolerance attitude towards drugs, as do many schools. You can't hold me to blame if they decide to take the programs elsewhere."

"I can," said Georgie, "and I do. You sit on the board of several schools, and you're on the board of companies where members influence schools. The Old Boys network. I know that you were behind many of those schools choosing to withdraw their programs from Chris Moore. And then, of course, the word got around, so other schools withdrew as well. A good reputation is a valuable thing, Jesse, and you knew that. This was no more than petty revenge."

"You're wrong."

"I'm not wrong. But I'm not going to argue with you about it. I'm offering you a choice. Undo what you have done. That will involve financial compensation for lost income, and you need to get those schools talking to Chris Moore again, get them to start rescheduling their outdoor programs. You need to talk to them and persuade them that he was a victim in all of this. Tell them that Harrison got caught up, as many young boys do, in events beyond his control." She raised her eyebrows at him. "We both know that's not true, that Harrison is out of control. But honestly, I don't care *what* you say—as long as you fix what you've done."

"You're asking a lot for someone who is not even an

Australian national," Jesse said. "Do you have a license for this?" He nodded around at their surroundings, his eyes alighting on the crystal ball again.

"Don't even go there, Jesse," Georgie said. "As I said, I have contacts. Right now, I'm prepared to trade what I know for you making things right again for Chris Moore. And it has to start happening within the week."

A muscle twitched in Jesse's jaw. He glared at her and then stared over her shoulder, clearly thinking of the best way out of this. "And if I decide that you and your demands are a load of psychic rubbish, what then?"

"Then I make sure that what I know filters out to the press," Georgie said. "You stand to lose a lot of money if it gets out that you were behind that heritage listing being hidden. And that's just for starters."

After trying to stare her down for thirty seconds, Jesse stood up. "You were right when you said that I have contacts. Many people have found, to their sorrow, that they would have done better to leave well alone. I don't forgive easily."

"No," said Georgie, "I realize that, having learned something about your tactics. Harrison is fine where he at the moment at his rehab center, but you can't keep hiding what he has done forever." She stared at him again. "Setting fire to the Moores' boat? And then having him raced off by a couple of your "employees"? I don't know if that would go down too well with the police, since Chris had to file an insurance claim. I'm sure they'd like to find out who was responsible."

"Harrison had nothing to do with that," Jesse said unconvincingly.

"I have a copy of the messages between you and your private investigators," Georgie said, staring up at him. "Don't make me go into detail, Jesse. I have plenty, and I'll use it. And just in case you're thinking of coming after me or the Moores, forget it. I'm not the only one that knows about this. If you start pushing it, you're going to regret it. I promise you that."

Angrily, Jesse kicked the chair he had been sitting on out of the way, at which it fell over with a clatter. Behind him, the curtain opened enough to let Scott slip inside. As he'd promised, he had stayed alert for any trouble.

Jesse turned around and saw him, and his lip curled. "You don't need to worry. I'm a respected member of the community. I'm hardly likely to assault a woman."

"That's good to know." Scott's usually good-humored voice was cold, his face unfriendly. "All done, now Georgie?"

"Yes, we're done." Georgie nodded at Jesse. "I'll give you one week, Mr. Burns. After that, I'll be expecting Chris to have news that schools have made contact. An apology from you wouldn't go astray either." She thought for a second and added, "And by the way, Chris Moore doesn't know anything about all of this. Nor does his son. And what they don't know, they can't tell."

He pushed past Scott, who didn't move, and then turned to look at Georgie as he was about to go out of the door. "My wife's pendant," he snapped. "Do you know where it is?"

"I have a fair idea," she said. "And if you do the right thing by Chris, I might be persuaded to let you know."

He skewered her with one last glare and disappeared

outside. Georgie could hear him asking the cameraman if he had received some useful information.

She didn't care what his response was.

"You okay?" Scott came over to her and wrapped his arms around her, resting his cheek on the top of her head. "He looked as though he would like to dismember you or string you up somewhere."

"Well, you didn't expect that he would like it, did you?" Georgie laughed, but her heart was beating fast.

"You're trembling." Scott rubbed her back. "Did he threaten you?"

"No more than I expected. I think he'll cooperate, though. He's got too much to lose. And I told him that there were a few people who knew about it, so there's no point in him trying to silence me." Georgie let out a long trembling sigh. "What is it about people like that? Why do they think they can just ride roughshod over everyone to get what they want?"

"They'll always be around, Georgie." Scott rocked her back and forth. "But we can help counter it a little bit. And then there are people like Bluey and the others he works for—whoever the hell they are. Eventually, most people like Burns get caught."

"I know. It's just… the people they hurt along the way."

"Come on." Scott picked up her bag from the back of the chair, slid the crystal ball inside, and handed it to her. "Let's go find Allie, tell her it's done. Then you're going to finish breakfast before you start delighting the masses with Gypsy Georgie."

Allie. The thought of her made Georgie smile. She would be so happy to hear good news. She wouldn't go into detail: it was better that the Moores didn't know all of it. For them, it would be enough to know that things were going to change.

And as for Drew, it was up to him whether he wanted to tell his father more about his role in it all.

29

End Game

"I'm going with you," Scott said in a tone that brooked no argument. "I don't trust that bloke."

"That's fine. I want you with me."

"You've taken more risks than usual, this time. We might think we have him, but cornered animals can get vicious." He snagged the car keys out of the bowl on the table.

"True," Georgie allowed, picking up her bag and following him out to the car. "But he's afraid of what else we might know. If he thinks he can make it all go away by schmoozing with his old schoolmates and throwing a bit of cash at Chris, he'll jump at it. It's just pocket change to him."

"Still." Scott still wore a frown as he started the car. "He'll make a bad enemy."

"But we're leaving in a couple of days," Georgie reminded him. "I'll make sure he knows I want nothing more to do with him. By the time everything collapses around him, we'll be long gone. He'll have far more to worry about than some dodgy business with one heritage building."

"Hmm." Turning the car towards Vincentia, Scott threw a glance her way. "After this, we're just going to noodle along and see the country for a while. Pure relaxation. No crystal ball. No detective work. And no criminals."

"I'm on board with that," Georgie said sunnily, treating him to a wide grin.

He looked at her suspiciously. "That was too easy."

"I've consulted the crystal ball," she assured him. "Nothing to see but beaches, gently rolling waves, and lazing about in deck chairs."

"Just one thing wrong with that," Scott pointed out. "We're heading inland. You *should* have been seeing red earth, scrub, and kangaroos."

Georgie put her seat back, wriggled into a comfortable position, and pushed her sunglasses up more firmly on her nose. "Oops. Wrong again."

"And you pass yourself off as an eight-generation gypsy?"

"As I keep telling everyone," she said, "it's not an exact science." She reached over and patted him on the knee. "Don't worry. I'm just as keen as you to play tourist for a while. After we see Jesse, we can draw a line under this and head off into the wild blue yonder."

"We'll see," said Scott. "We'll see."

Jesse Burns had clearly decided to play the role of an upstanding and unfairly treated citizen, stiffly polite but cold. They all knew what lay beneath, but Georgie was happy to follow his lead. She would rather endure this version of Jesse than the stone-cold thug that lay beneath his private-school veneer.

He met them at the door and led them into the sitting room, where his wife stood at the expansive glass windows staring out at the waves lapping the beach. Clad in expensive casual clothes with subtle designer labels, strappy sandals on her feet, and her blonde hair artistically mussed, she looked as though she'd just stepped out of a photoshoot for *Marie Claire*.

At the sound of their footsteps, she turned to face them, making no attempt to hide her disdain.

"This is my wife, Jenna," Jesse said. "Jenna, may I introduce you to Georgie and Scott?"

Georgie didn't care for the spite in his voice, but then, she wasn't here to make friends. Or to change his opinion of her.

"Pleased to meet you," she said. Scott nodded.

"So you're the gypsy fortune-teller," Jenna said, looking her up and down. "Jesse says you know where my pendant is."

"I may do," Georgie said. *Keep up that attitude, lady, and you'll never find out where.*

Jesse walked forward, put a hand on his wife's arm, and gave her a meaningful look. "We'll get to that in a moment, Jenna. Let's all sit down."

Georgie and Scott perched together on the edge of the cream-colored sofa while Jenna took an armchair opposite them. She crossed her legs and stared straight at Georgie, swinging one foot.

Jesse picked up a folder and crossed to Georgie. "Here. You should find this satisfactory."

Georgie opened it. It was an accountant's estimate of the money that *Moore Kayaks and Canoes* should have earned, dating from the school trip that had gone so wrong last year, with a total in red and something called 'goodwill bonus' added. That, she assumed, would be what might have been an adjustment in court for pain and suffering. But what Jesse Burns had done to the Moores would never get to court, and the 'bonus' didn't make up for what he'd put them through.

Still, it was better than nothing.

Wondering how Jesse had obtained those figures, she passed it to Scott. "What do you think?"

He skimmed the estimates, stared off to one side while he did his own mental calculations, and then nodded. "Fair enough." He looked at Jesse and echoed Georgie's thoughts. "You based this on the school programs that were withdrawn, I assume?"

"Something like that. Keep reading," said Jesse.

Georgie flipped the page over and read the letter underneath. It was addressed to *Moore Kayaks and Canoes*, and in formal language, expressed Jesse Burns' opinion that the business may have suffered unnecessarily through no fault of its staff after an 'unfortunate incident' involving his son. As someone who had worked for years to sponsor local businesses and encourage growth, he went on, he wished to make this gesture to show his support for a highly-respected member of the community and assist him in coming back from a downturn.

There was one more sheet of paper in the folder. Georgie glanced at it and felt a surge of relief. It listed half a dozen private schools in Sydney, with contact details for their outdoor program coordinators.

She looked at him. "This last sheet of paper. Does that mean you've contacted all these schools?"

"It means I've been in touch with people who have

influence," he said unsmilingly. "They've made the necessary phone calls. Those schools will all confirm outdoor programs with Moore within the next week if they haven't already."

"Okay," she said. "How will you get the money to him?"

"He already has it," Burns said. "Direct deposit. I got the details from his wife." He bit off the word *'wife'*. "And I've had my secretary mail the letter."

Good, thought Georgie. Allie would be sensible about accepting the money as being no more than they were entitled due. If Burns had contacted Chris, he'd be likely to have his offer thrown back in his face.

She nodded and stood up. "I think we're done, then."

"Not quite," Jesse said. "Two things more." His gaze grew colder.

Scott, also standing up, moved closer and took her elbow as Georgie waited for him to go on.

"The first thing," Jesse said. "This means we're quits. You don't mention to anyone what we talked about on the day of the markets. *Ever.*"

"You don't need to threaten me, Mr. Burns," Georgie said quietly. "We agreed that I wouldn't go to the media with what I know, and that still stands. I have no further interest in you and your activities."

"And I'll hold you to that," he said. "I wouldn't want you to be looking over your shoulder for the rest of your life."

Georgie's pulse speeded up, but she managed not to betray the stab of anxiety at his words. "We're in agreement about that, too. What's the second thing?" She felt

Scott's fingers tighten on her arm and appreciated it that he didn't step in like a lot of men would have.

"The pendant," Jenna spat at her, leaning forward. "It's worth far more to me than that piddling little payment to Chris Moore. Where is it?"

Georgie looked from one to the other and thought about the kind of people who worried more about diamond pendants and power than simple kindness. She thought about Jason Hoy with his greasy hair and his part-time drugs business and Chad Royston passing himself off as a respectable personal trainer while he channeled drugs to school kids and peddled steroids on the side.

Let Jesse Burns do what he had to, to get his precious pendant back from Chad Royston. They deserved each other.

"Your pendant," she said, "is probably in a shoebox hidden somewhere in Chad Royston's garage. *Probably.* If he's sold it or moved it, then don't blame me."

She turned and walked out, with Jenna's outraged cry echoing in her ears.

30

Celebrations

ALLIE WOULDN'T HEAR of them leaving town without coming over for a thank-you barbecue. "Surf and turf," she told Georgie on the phone. "Big juicy t-bones from the local butcher and fresh king prawns. We're celebrating."

Georgie accepted willingly. "Sounds great. I'll bring the wine."

"Emma and Drew are coming too," Allie said happily. "I've got news to tell you about them, too. Wait until you hear."

"You're not going to tell me that I got it wrong and Emma's having triplets, are you?"

"Wait until you get here," Allie said. "Say five o'clock? We'll eat at around six so it's not a late night; I know you want to hit the road early."

Drew beckoned Georgie aside not long after she and Scott arrived, seizing a moment when his mother and

Emma were in the kitchen and his father was busy at the barbecue. "Can I speak with you for a moment?"

"Sure." They wandered down the grassy slope and stood at the water's edge, watching the late afternoon light on the water and a few boats puttering around the corner to the jetty at Sussex Inlet.

"I finally told Ma how it all went down," Drew said abruptly. "She thinks I should wait a bit before telling Dad, once things settle down."

"Well, she's been married to him for over a quarter of a century, so she should know." Georgie smiled at him gently. "I bet her reaction wasn't as bad as you'd expected."

He bent down, picked up a pebble and tossed it into the water. "No. She can see how it happened." He shook his head. "No wonder high school kids get sucked in. With me it was 'a few harmless stimulants to bring you to peak performance', and then steroids, and then a few ecstasy tablets just for fun…then it's 'just try this, it won't hurt you'…" He turned to face her. "I was lucky, in a way, that this all happened. After that Harrison business I just quit, cold turkey."

Georgie asked him a question that had been on her mind. "Do you think Jason and Chad deliberately set you up?"

"I've gone over it a million times, and now I think… yes, probably." He stared out across the water. "That was the first thing Emma said, actually, once she got over the shock. It was a bit too convenient, using me, wasn't it?"

"That's what Scott and I thought, too, when we talked it over," Georgie admitted. "Jason *lives* with him, yet he calls you the night before and gives *you* the stuff to hand over to him when you pick up the steroids?"

"Chad said Jason was spending the night down at the camp—just going to pick up the kids from the camp the next day, drop them off at the launch point, and then take the bus back to base." Drew hooked his thumbs in the belt loops of his shorts. "I thought: well, he's just driving the bus, so he's not going to be taking drugs onto the water with the kids. But obviously, after I gave them to him, he handed them straight over to Harrison Burns." He shook his head. "Then he took off, and the rest of us were left to handle the mess."

"Did you confront Jason about it, later?"

"Yes. At first he denied giving them to the Burns kid. Then he just told me to shut up about it or it would come out that I was the one responsible for bringing the drugs in—and that would see the end of Dad's business for sure."

"And Harrison? He didn't finger either Jason or you?"

"And risk his supply? No chance of that."

Quick footsteps sounded behind them, and Emma bounced up. "Hey, you two! Come up and be sociable. We've got celebrating to do!"

Drew smiled at her and threw an arm around her shoulders. "We sure have. I was just filling in Georgie."

"I thought as much." Impulsively, Emma leaned over and kissed Georgie on the cheek. "Thanks for all you've done for us. For the family."

"It was my pleasure," Georgie said, feeling a lump in her throat. "I'm so glad things worked out. New baby, new business—" She stopped. "I'm guessing that's the big news Allie is planning to tell me about? You're going into business with your Dad?"

"Yep," Drew said. "So act surprised."

"Drew," Georgie said with a wink, "I'm a gypsy fortune-teller. Your mother probably thinks I already know anyway."

As she walked up the slope with Drew on one side, looking as though a weight had lifted from his shoulders, and a beaming Emma on the other, she looked up and saw the other three around the barbecue. Allie had an arm around her husband's waist, looking up at him and laughing as he checked the gas supply for the barbecue. Chris looked back at her and dropped a kiss on her nose, looking somehow taller and more determined. Like a man who could see he had a future again.

And Scott. Darling Scott, her rock and companion.

She walked up to him and linked her arm in his, thinking: *Red earth, waterholes and kangaroos. We're on our way.*

No criminals. No mysteries to solve.

At least for a few weeks.

From the Author

Sussex Inlet is a sleepy little haven beloved of the boating fraternity and fishermen—and scuba divers who like to explore the pristine waters of Jervis Bay and St Georges Basin. It's a lovely area, and many holiday makers choose to stay in the local campgrounds or tourist parks. Huskisson, where Georgie and Scott stayed, has a delightful white beach you'll love to visit.

Hyams Beach is a small area of prosperous homes, not far from Vincentia. To the best of my knowledge nobody named Jesse Burns lives there, and there's no Chad Royston or Jason Hoy in Sussex Inlet. Nor is there a private school called White Sands College!

Ah, an author's imagination is a wonderful thing!

I hope you enjoyed this story. As Scott says, he and Georgie are heading inland, for red earth and water-holes and wildlife. They're planning to just relax for a while…

…but you know Georgie. ;-)

Have you read Rosa's story yet? Join my newsletter subscribers to download this free ebook. You'll find out more about Georgie and her family…and see where she got her special gift!

MargMcAlister.com/free-georgie-book

I also like to write to my readers with snippets of upcoming books and inside information about Georgie's world!

ABOUT THE AUTHOR

Marg McAlister is the author of the popular Georgie B. Goode Cozy Mystery series (set in the USA) and Series 2 (Australian RV Adventure series), also featuring Georgie.

Marg lives by the sea on the mid-north coast of NSW, but she and her husband spend part of the year on The Gemfields in Central Queensland, living off the grid on their mining claim. While her husband digs for sapphires and zircons, operates the wash plant and drives around dirt tracks, Marg is usually writing—or socializing!

Marg is also the author of a series of books for aspiring writers, and the owner of Blue Gem Publishing, which publishes books in a range of genres.

Glossary

Georgie is swiftly becoming accustomed to the way Australians speak, but sometimes people from other countries can be scratching their heads at Australian idioms and contractions. So here's a translation for you of some of the common terms used in this book!

Ambo — ambulance officer, paramedic

Air con — air conditioning

Arvo — afternoon

Australian States and Territories:

QLD — Queensland

NSW — New South Wales

VIC — Victoria

TAS (or "Tassie") — Tasmania

SA — South Australia

WA — Western Australia

NT — Northern Territory

ACT — Australian Capital Territory (in NSW)

Aussie, Oz — shortened form of Australia

Back-burning — creating a fire break

Big Banana — tourist attraction and information Center near Coffs Harbour, New South Wales

Bloke — man, guy

Bluey — common nickname for any male with red hair

Boardwalk — a timber walkway which can be built over rocks, sand or the forest floor

Bushfire — brush fire, wildfire, forest fire

Caravan — travel trailer

Cuppa — cup of tea

Chook — slang for chicken, also the nickname of the Bad Guy in Book 1 of the Australian RV Series

Fireys — Firemen - an affectionate term for volunteers who fight fires with the Rural Fire Service

Grey Nomads — retirees who travel around the country in RVs

Hi-vis — bright yellow or orange safety clothing, often fluorescent

Ice — crystal methamphetamine

Jayco — common brand of RVs

LandCruiser — 4WD Toyota LandCruiser, a popular choice to tow caravans in Australia

Macca's — McDonalds Fast Food restaurant

Newsagent — newsstand

Nurofen, Nurofen Plus — painkiller tablets

paddock — a field

Panadol — similar to paracetamol & Tylenol - a common brand of painkiller in Australia

RFS — Rural Fire Service (a volunteer organization to fight the bushfires that rage in Australia every summer)

Staghorn fern — (also elk horn) a treetop fern that

has evolved to grow in the Australian rainforest; does not need soil

Scrub turkey — the Australian Brush-turkey. It has black body plumage, a bare red head and yellow throat wattle

Tradie — tradesman, anyone with a trade

Ute — utility truck or pickup

Waeco fridge — a common brand of portable fridge (car fridge)

Water dragon — a lizard that can stay submerged for up to an hour

www.ingramcontent.com/pod-product-compliance
Lightning Source LLC
Chambersburg PA
CBHW020806190726
48285CB00006B/2173